Circle Games

Jo Mazelis was born and still lives in Swansea. Her first short fiction collection, *Diving Girls*, was shortlisted for the ACW Book of the Year Award and the Commonwealth Writers' Award. She has won the Rhys Davies Award three times and her work has appeared widely in magazines and anthologies, and has been broadcast on BBC Radio Four.

A selection of stories from *Circle Games* and *Diving Girls*, in Danish translation, is forthcoming from Forlaget Arvids.

Circle Games

Jo Mazelis

Parthian
The Old Surgery
Napier Street
Cardigan
SA43 1ED

www.parthianbooks.co.uk

First published in 2005
© Jo Mazelis 2005
All Rights Reserved

ISBN 1-902638-58-1
ISBN 9 781902 638584

Editor: Gwen Davies

Inner design by type@lloydrobson.com
Cover design and photograph by Jo Mazelis
Printed and bound by Dinefwr Press, Llandybïe, Wales

Published with the financial support of the Welsh Books
Council

British Library Cataloguing in Publication Data –
A cataloguing record for this book is available from the
British Library

This book is for K

Contents

We can be richer than industry
As long as we know
That there's things that
We don't really need
Willie Mason – *Oxygen*

Depression is the flaw in love. To be creatures who love, we
must be creatures who despair at what we lose.
Andrew Solomon – *The Noonday Demon*

Children, be curious. Nothing is worse (I know it) than when
curiosity stops. Nothing is more repressive than the repression
of curiosity. Curiosity begets love. It weds us to the world.
Graham Swift – *Waterland*

For the Angels

It was his turn to pick up the child from school, and he resented it. Or at least he didn't resent it as far as his daughter was concerned, but in terms of the timing and the disruption to his schedule and who the favour was for, he burned with resentment. Not that he showed it.

'Hey, sweetie,' he said as soon as he caught sight of his daughter.

'Daddy!' she said, and then she put her two arms into the air, palms outstretched, which meant 'carry me!' He pretended he didn't understand this message as his back was playing up.

The kids were spilling out of the school all around them, and the other parents, mothers mostly, formed a sort of counter offensive, taking stations by the high gates, blocking the entrance with their tracksuit-bottomed, sloppy-shoed selves. You could always spot the stay-at-home mothers; they tended to be frowsy, overweight, and whatever brains they'd had were extinguished by years of 'Get yer coat on, where's yer gym kit, what do you mean "homework" you little bugger, you never cowing said last night'.

He bent down to hug his daughter, and gave her a peck on the cheek, which she returned by squeezing his neck and pressing her mouth to a spot below his eye while she made a loud and enthusiastic 'mmm-ah' kissing noise.

'Alright then,' he said, embarrassed, 'that's enough, 'kay?'

He straightened himself, took the child's hand and began threading his way past the other parents and children.

'Where's your car, Daddy?'

'S'down here, on a side street, a bit of a way.'

'Why?'

'Why? Well, 'cos there's so many other bloody cars blocking the road by the school.'

She was skipping along by his side. Six years old, prettiest little thing, big dark spaniel eyes, gleaming mahogany hair, button nose, soft round cheeks that always had a rosy glow to them. 'Little Miss Heart Breaker' was what he sometimes called her.

Lately though, he'd noticed that she was getting a wee bit plump. She'd been a delicate 6lb 3oz baby; but now she seemed to be heavier than other kids her age; she had a sort of stolidness, a gravity, and there were still dimples on the backs of her hands and you had no sense of any bone structure, just this plump fleshiness.

2

'Where do you want to go for tea?' he asked her.

'Umm,' she put a finger to her lip to demonstrate that she was thinking.

'Well?'

'I'll whisper,' she said, tugging at his hand to make him stop.

He rolled his eyes theatrically heavenward then lowered himself on to his haunches so that he was at her level.

She leaned against him and he could feel the awkward weight of her, her lack of grace. She fumbled with his hair, cupped his ear and breathed heavily before whispering the name of his local pub.

He straightened himself and felt buoyant all of a sudden, like he could walk on water or something. He scooped his daughter up and plonked her onto his hip and she held on like a fat little monkey as he strode to the car.

He'd actually driven around the school twice before he finally admitted defeat and manoeuvered the car into a space on Robinson Road. The street gave him the willies. A row of elegant yellow brick semi-detached villas stretched along the left hand side of the road, while on the right, opposite the homes was a graveyard. The graveyard must have been about two, maybe three acres, and the part that faced the street was on a hill that rolled upwards, so that all you would see, if you lived there and if you glanced from the front windows, would be gravestones, row upon row of them, stretching off in every direction: regimented, pale, cold stone interrupted here and there by splashes of bright colour where people had left fresh flowers.

'Look, Daddy, look!' his daughter said with rising excitement in her voice. He had been avoiding looking to the right but now his daughter was insisting he look that way. She was even trying to force his head physically to turn, pushing against his left cheek with the flat of her hand, digging her knee into his rib cage as if he were a horse.

'Alright! Whoa!' he stopped and bent his knees so that she could clamber off.

She was pointing towards the graveyard, except that because she was lower down she could no longer see whatever it was she wanted to show him, and so she was hopping from one foot to the other and craning her neck.

There was only a low hedge separating the pavement from the cemetery, but it was enough to block her view.

'This way Daddy, c'mon,' she pulled his hand, guiding him across the road as if he was blind. There was a metal gate enclosed in a half circle of railing like a swing door, which was meant to be animal proof, though there were plenty of gaps in the railing and hedge that were big enough for even a large dog to get through.

'Oh, what d'you want to go there for?' he asked wearily.

'Come on, Daddy, I'll show you.'

'One minute,' he said, 'that's it. Otherwise the pub'll be shut.'

He lied to her habitually, without even thinking about it, because that was how you managed children, wasn't it? Except that every now and then she surprised him by seeing through his lies, as she did now.

'No, it won't,' she said emphatically, 'silly Daddy!'

'There's only gravestones in there. You know what those are, don't you?'

By the way of an answer she pulled harder on his hand and he let himself be led through the gate. The first thing he noticed once they were inside was a heap of rubbish behind a yew tree. There was a largish wire mesh bin, but rubbish spilled out from it and had been heaped around it. Most of it consisted of dead flowers, but some of them were arranged in complicated displays and one of the largest spelled out DAD. On the bare earth, not more than a few inches away, a used condom lay coiled in the mud like a shed skin.

'Look, Daddy, look!'

He glanced around, letting his eye rove over the strange landscape, wondering what it was she wanted him to see. His daughter was staring at the row of graves that ran parallel with the hedge opposite the houses.

'See?'

He couldn't see anything, or certainly not anything that would excite the child in this way.

'Oh yeah,' he said, but his voice had a dead note in it that didn't ring true. It was like the sound his voice had made when things got bad in the marriage.

'Is everything alright?' his ex used to ask.

'Yeah,' he'd say, shrugging.

'Are you happy?'

'Yeah.'

'But you don't seem happy.'

'Oh sorry, but you can't expect a person to be ecstatically happy all the time. I'm tired. I'm pissed off with my job, the car's a wreck, the house is a mess, we're broke and now I have to listen to all this bloody talk about happiness. I'm still here, aren't I?'

It was hardly the most reassuring of speeches but maybe if he'd just ended it with a kiss, a whispered 'I'm sorry', instead of what he usually did when she started in on him, which was to walk out of the house and down the road to the pub.

Usually by the time he got back at maybe nine or ten o'clock, she'd be red-eyed and penitent. She'd put his dinner in the microwave and he'd sit obediently picking at it, but he always had the sensation that he was eating leftovers, and he prided himself on having nothing secondhand.

He glanced down at his daughter; she was standing transfixed with her little chin lifted and her hands clasped together over her chest. Her pose was almost theatrical, the sort of thing you'd see a child actor do in an advert when they saw a dolphin or Santa or bloody Tinkerbell. It seemed more learned than natural, an adult's idea of how wonderment should look for a child.

'Alright,' he said, 'that's enough.'

'Oh, but Daddy look, isn't she beautiful?'

He trained his eye over the gravestones again. Weeds. Dirty neglected stones. The odd wooden cross lolling at a demented angle. Flat granite stones that had cracked and half sunk into the earth like something from a horror film. Names, pious sentiments. Endless references to sleep and love and greatly missed. And dates and ages. Aged 3. Aged 92. Aged 38. His age. Her age. For Edna our beloved daughter who went to God's side.

He was barely listening to what his daughter said. He was aware that she was speaking, but a part of him was content to just hear it as babble. Sweet, he was sure, sweet in its pitch and musicality, but without significance as far as meaning was concerned. He had registered vaguely that his daughter had said something; a 'she' of some sort was beautiful, but he took that to be a female animal; a puppy perhaps, or a squirrel or maybe a bird.

There was a bird busily hopping around vaguely in the direction the child was looking, but it was a bloody ugly thing, a crow with a heavy looking beak, black and stark and moving clumsily, almost mechanically, and who knew if it was a 'he' or a 'she'?

He put his hand on his daughter's shoulder in order to guide her back towards the car, but she stood firm, wouldn't budge even when he increased the pressure of his hand.

'C'mon, we can't stand here all night.'

'Why?'

'Why!'

'Yes. Why?'

'Because the man won't let us.'

'What man?'

'The man who looks after the graves.'

'Where?'

'Come on, you're being silly.'

'But you haven't seen her.'

'Yes, I have.'

'No, you haven't.'

But he wasn't listening, he made one last effort to tug the child from her spot, then said, 'Right, I'm going to count to four then I'm going back to the car. One. Two...'

The child folded her arms and lowered her head.

'You're a mean Daddy,' she informed him.

'Three...'

'I don't like you.'

'Fine, what do I care? Four!' and with that he turned his back on her, and at a slow, forgiving pace, he made for the gate.

He didn't want to look behind him. He certainly never remembered his parents turning back to look at him when he was a child, but he well remembered his own breathless teary panic as he tried to keep up with them. His father in one of the loud check sports jackets he favoured; his mother swathed in psychedelic floral swirls that made her look even fatter than she really was. The pair of them oblivious to him.

'I'm walking away,' he thought, 'I'm turning my back,' and it seemed that his footsteps became alien; dislocated and phony. He was strangely aware of his back, aware of it in the way that one is when watching a scary movie. When you turned your back on a thing, he thought, you never knew what might happen.

His slow pace allowed him to listen for movement. He expected his daughter to follow him. That was how the trick of walking away worked, the child had to believe they were being deserted; that the parent would really walk away, get in their car and drive off. Maybe there was a limit to the number of times you could pull that trick. Eventually the child would see through it, would appreciate their own power, the terrible and engulfing love of a parent for a child.

His ears strained to hear the soft tiptoe sounds of his daughter and for a while he heard nothing, then as he neared the gate he heard her. Yes, there was movement, not very close to him, but she was moving.

He had to push the swinging gate forward before he entered the semi-circle of railing, and the metal was rusted and the hinges unoiled so that it rattled and creaked and clanged in protest. He manoeuvered his way through and just before he stepped onto the pavement he looked back at the graveyard. He fully expected to see his child ten or maybe fifteen feet away on the gravel path, but there was no sign of her.

'Emma!' he called out instinctively, his voice sharp and ringing in the empty air.

Silence.

He could feel panic rising in him, mixed with anger, 'Emma, I'm telling you, come here now!'

'Jesus Christ,' he murmured under his breath, and he found his mind was off, racing through a hundred terrible thoughts that he could neither subdue nor bear.

'Em-ma!'

His pulse raced and his heart pounded. His palms grew clammy. There was movement to his right and he raced towards it, but as he neared the spot, instead of Emma, he saw that same ugly crow. It jerked itself into the air as if tugged upward by invisible wires, flapped its wings, cawing wildly. He wanted to throw a damn rock at it and would have except that he had more pressing matters at hand.

So he swore at it instead; cursed it, not that the bird seemed to care, it just turned its back and waddled off, stiff-legged.

As he watched it, he heard a child's laugh that was somehow both unfamiliar and yet instantly recognizable. He turned sharply in the direction of the sound and saw a flash of pale turquoise moving behind the gravestones near the hedge.

Keeping his eye on the spot, he walked down the path again.

'Okay, enough is enough.'

He paused and gazed down the row. Emma popped her head out, but only long enough for him to see the mischievous grin.

'I see you,' he called, relaxing at last, 'come on, love, we've got to go.' His voice was calm, warm, forgiving.

'No.'

'What?'

'No.'

She was about thirty feet away; they had to raise their voices. How strange it must sound, he thought, their two voices, calling across a graveyard, echoing off stones, lost and ghostly under a lowering sky.

'This isn't funny,' he said, and by way of reply she giggled, but the laugh had a false note in it. Like she was learning a new language of appeasement, but couldn't resist irony.

'Damn stubborn child,' he hissed under his breath and flapped his arms helplessly against his sides. He wanted to say how 'the man' would come soon, how then she'd be sorry. But she'd seen through that one already.

'If I have to come there...' he said, letting warning dance on his tongue, 'you'll be sorry.' He waited, thinking how this was her mother's doing, how she was too damn soft with the child. 'Em-ma. I mean it.'

'Come and see,' she called out then, a sort of triumph in her voice.

What was his problem anyway? Would he have felt as unreasonably angry at her antics if they'd been in a park or at the beach? It just seemed indecent somehow to play hide and seek amongst the dead. And he'd had this thing; this fear since he was so high, that if you stepped on a grave, something really bad would happen; something seriously bad and unstoppable. And in these damn neglected graveyards you never knew, once you got off the path, where one grave stopped and another started.

He took a deep breath, then stepped from the path and headed down the tangled row towards his daughter. He made slow progress, checking where he placed each foot as carefully as if he was in a minefield.

Emma was standing out in the open now, waiting for him, watching as he came nearer. Her face wore a look of almost adult patience, as if she were the parent watching a child taking his first faltering steps. And he felt grateful suddenly; in a way he never imagined he could, grateful to her just for being herself, for being this strange and infinitely small, infinitely wonderful human being. He had a sense suddenly of the sort of woman she would someday be, the casual strength she'd carry in her whole being.

Years later he'd dream about this, except that in the dreams as soon as he reached her she would disappear.

But she was there that day, sure enough, in her turquoise coat and navy school skirt, with dimples in her cheeks, her knees, on the backs of her hands, watching him, waiting.

'Okay,' he said as he finally drew level with her, 'let's see it.' All his anger had left him now, but he still injected the hard-done-by tone into his voice, just to stress the fact that she'd pushed him, she'd got her way. Again.

'Isn't it pretty?' she said and pointed upward.

It was only then he saw it, and it seemed incredible to him that he hadn't seen it before now. Jesus, he must have a screw loose, he must be blind to have not seen it. It wasn't something you could miss. An angel carved from white stone; marble maybe or onyx, an angel with huge outstretched wings and feet that seemed to almost float, so cunningly were they done. An angel with a face that seemed both bland and beautiful, human and not human.

'Whoa,' he said.

'You couldn't see her,' the child informed him, 'but now you can.'

'Well, yeah,' he said, 'but I was looking for you, that's why.'

And with that he took a step backwards to better see the statue, and his foot met with the flat stone of a grave instead of earth, but somehow it no longer mattered.

Meeting Her

The first time Alec saw the girl of his dreams he had to crawl through a long narrow tunnel of rainbow-coloured silk in order to reach her. The tunnel was part of an installation artwork called Loop de Loop. It was the strangest place to fall in love.

The morning this happened was an overcast Tuesday and a fine drizzle had been saturating the city for two days. November, and the municipal Christmas lights were already up in the shopping centre and streets. His neighbours, the Nevilles, had begun to put up their own lavish decorations on the outside of their home. They put up more decorations every year; leaping reindeer, glowing laughing Santas on the walls, white dripping icicle lights hanging from the guttering. This year they'd got hold of some plastic tube lights that looped and bent into any shape you fancied and they had this zigzagging up and down every inch of spare wall. Last year they had tried to persuade him to let them add his part of the property to their seasonal attractions.

The house had once been a large and rambling Victorian home; creamy yellow bricks with gables and complicated carved wooden trim. Then the house was divided into two and sold off, and as soon as the Nevilles moved in they had modernised their half with white plastic windows, and re-rendered the walls in a pinkish pebble dash. Alec had maintained the original features, even though the wooden sash windows needed constant repainting and some of the wooden trim was disintegrating into a rotten pulp in places.

That Tuesday the Nevilles had been out on the front lawn at eight in the morning erecting a six-foot high 'thing'. He thought of it as a 'thing' partly because his view of it gave no clue as to what it was. He had squinted out through his curtains when he heard the hammering and the voices, in time to see a flat piece of chipboard being propped against a wooden framework. The thing was shaped like a curious sort of mountain range.

He had dressed quickly, partly from rage at being woken so early and partly from curiosity. He'd slammed his front door and pounded, as much as one can pound on gravel, down the front path and out of the gate. He'd turned left instead of right onto the pavement so that he could eyeball the thing in the Neville's garden.

It was a life-size model of the crib. There was Joseph, tall, dark and bearded, standing guard, while Mary in the obligatory sky blue cloak knelt by the manger with her hands outstretched, palms upward. Behind her a toffee-coloured cow was breathing down her neck and next to her a lamb was taking a quick nap. The baby was blonde and blue-eyed and looked like it must be six months old at least.

'Jesus Christ!' Alec had muttered under his breath at the sight of it and then he'd stormed off with no particular place to go, but a strong urge to just walk off his anger before he returned home. That was why, at 10.30, he had found himself crawling through the multi-coloured tunnel in the disused church.

When he had got over his feelings about the absurdity of what he was doing, he rather enjoyed the crawl. The passage looped round and around in a spiral. At the entrance it had warned claustrophobics and epileptics not to enter, which he had thought was a little extreme, but when he was inside he could see that there was something unsettling and confusing about the experience. Once in, you were committed; there was no turning around, you could only move forward and the journey, because of the loops, seemed much longer than you might have expected.

He was grateful that he was the only person in the tube that day. The thought of other people shuffling along on their knees both behind and in front of him was unpleasant for all sorts of reasons, though he didn't dwell on them.

Near the centre the tunnel seemed to curve inward at a sharper degree, which meant that you saw less and less of the way ahead. He was just beginning to panic and feel like he would never reach the end when suddenly he found himself crowding into a sort of circular tent area. The floor here was soft; it must have been built over a mattress or something, and the walls were silky and grey like a shady dell. On one side there was a video screen, which seemed to be activated when you entered the cave. The screen blazed with a bluish white light and a woman's voice spoke.

'You are come at last,' she said, 'oh my lost one, how I have missed you, my love, my love.'

Slowly the figure of a woman appeared on the screen. She was sitting on a plastic chair in front of a window through which sunlight seemed to blaze. She did not speak, just gazed at the camera.

Alec settled himself more comfortably. He was waiting for her to speak again. Waiting for some explicit end to the artistic experience. He watched her face intently. She was around thirty he guessed, with dark shiny hair cut in a Louise Brooks style. A straight inoffensive nose, brown eyes, well-defined brows, nice kissable lips and pale flawless skin.

He waited, watching all the while. He could hear her breathing and the faint muffled sound of white noise. As nothing more seemed to be happening he shifted his position in readiness to head on and out, but as he moved she spoke.

'Don't go,' she said, 'don't leave me.'

He froze and waited again, watching her. She kept her eyes on the camera and then he saw that slowly, and with great subtlety, she was beginning to cry. Tears welled up in her eyes, making them shine and look even more beautiful, and her face wore an expression of indescribable sorrow.

The eyes swam and brimmed and she drew in a sharp breath. Tears trickled first from one eye then the other, and he watched their shining journey down her cheeks.

He was transfixed. It seemed so real. He wondered if the woman was an actress, but then hated the idea so much that he forced it from his mind. He thought instead that maybe the woman was in some sort of institute; that either she was insane or had just been told that she was dying.

That felt better. It definitely felt better; he did not want to be moved by phoney tears. And he was moved. Her sorrow made him not merely pity her, but ache for her. And rising from the ache, despite her disintegrating face, which was now red and fiery and distorted in a grimace, he felt a love. And, he reasoned, it was love. Not desire or lust, which would have been easily driven off by the terrible weeping.

Then the screen began to brighten, to grow whiter, dissolving her face in light. He almost cried out, 'Don't go!' but the sudden consciousness that she could neither see nor hear stopped him.

He watched the screen in the hope that she would be resurrected but there was only the white glare. He shifted his position in the hope that movement would trigger the video to restart. And, when that didn't work he shuffled backwards up the tunnel for a couple of yards then entered the grey cave again, but to no avail.

To the left of the video screen, there seemed to be an exit or the entrance to another tunnel, and with the hope that it was the latter, he moved on his knees towards it. There was a grey curtain and beyond, the gallery. The height of the room was somewhat of a shock. As was the ordinariness of the place, the bland and passionless cold light of day.

Depressed suddenly, and disappointed, he made for the exit. The passage led back to the foyer. Coming at it from the opposite side, he found it looked different, but then maybe it was he that was changed. He had rushed in when he arrived, his mind still buzzing with anger. The anger was now entirely dissipated and he could not even imagine why he had been so maddened by the Nevilles' excesses. If he didn't control himself, he would turn into an old curmudgeon, a twenty-first century Scrooge, pouring bitter scorn on his fellow men, on Christmas, on hope and love.

There was a poster for the exhibition on the wall, and the title, Loop de Loop was repeated in a circle so that it could be read as infinity. Beneath, he read the name of the artist, Bethan Matthews. Next to the poster was a row of laminated A4 sheets. He moved down the wall reading each of them. The first was a brief biography, the next a list of previous exhibitions and group shows and prizes. Then there were three pages about Loop de Loop.

'Bethan Matthews is interested in ideas about alienation and the eternal need for love. "It is a need that can never be fulfilled," the artist stated in an interview, "because what we seek is an escape from the prison of self. Art is more permanent than love."'

After that there was a lot of analysis, and references to Lacan and Cixous and even Walt Disney. He ran his eye over this, not really taking any of it in, but meaning to come back and reread it sometime.

He looked at the artist's biography again. She was born in 1977 on the island of Crete. Her mother was a poet, her father a musician who had drowned three days after her birth.

Alec looked at the list of her previous exhibitions. 'Absence', 'Ruby Slippers' and 'I'm Melting' all sounded, in the light of what he now knew, intriguing. The woman on the video screen was the artist. He should have known that and if he hadn't been in such a hurry, he would have read all this before. But maybe then he would have raised his defences, prepared himself for an onslaught of art with a capital A.

Not that he disliked art; it was just that it left him feeling raw. But the sensation came from the idea that he was missing the point, rather than the art itself. Though sometimes he considered that *that* must be the point, mustn't it?

He knew what most certainly wasn't art and that was the thing in the Nevilles' garden. Now, however, his earlier rage seemed absurd. Out of all proportion with the reality of the situation. He smiled when he remembered his fury and as he smiled a voice very close to him caused him to wheel around.

'Oh, I'm sorry, I didn't mean to scare you.'

'That's okay,' he said.

'You've seen the exhibition?'

'Ah, yes.'

'Hi, I'm Bethan Matthews,' she said and offered him her hand.

'Yes, yes, of course.'

She smiled.

'Did you like it?' she asked.

'Did I like it? Hmm...' he released her hand, '"like" is a funny word. It's like "nice", isn't it? Was it nice?'

'No,' she said 'I don't think that's so.'

'Hmm. Don't you think that "Do you like it?" sounds like something you'd say about a new dress, a new way of cooking potatoes?'

She sighed, 'Well, I didn't really want to get into a big quarrel over semantics. So let's put the question another way. Did you hate it then?'

'Oh, god, no. No, no, no!'

'No, you didn't hate it?'

'I definitely didn't hate it. It. Umm...' he wanted to explain that he had felt moved, but he couldn't explain, and the language that came to mind was the language of love, not art. Finally after a great deal of hesitation he managed to say that it was 'interesting' and 'thought provoking'.

She looked displeased by this, as if he was challenging her in some obscure and insulting way.

She was smaller than he imagined, more delicate and childlike than she appeared on the video. He smiled helplessly at her.

'Well, anyway,' she said, 'I've got a questionnaire here and I've been asking people to fill it in. Would you? It only takes a couple of minutes.'

He nodded his assent, and she led him to a bench and handed him the papers.

The questions were straightforward enough on the first page: gender, age, occupation and so on. For this last he was torn between writing 'architect' because that was what he was qualified to do and 'unemployed' which was his current state. He decided on the latter, though he did wonder which answer would appeal to her more.

If he'd had trouble with the simple question of 'occupation' the next page would seem almost impossible. The questions were: 'Have you ever been in love? Are you in love now? Are you happy? Do you feel yourself to be alone?'

He glanced up from the page and saw Bethan Matthews sitting on the other side of the foyer. She was reading a book. He wrote down 'yes' to every question. The next sheet had just one question, but a whole blank space in which to answer.

'What is art?' he read, and to which he wrote, 'you are' which he thought was rather clever.

The last sheet also had only one question and a big space. 'How did 'Loop de Loop' make you feel?'

'It made me fall in love with you,' he wrote or rather scrawled messily across the page. He underlined the statement five times. Then as an afterthought he added in a modest sized print 'I'd like to see you in the real world – call me – 624681, Alec.'

Then he gathered the sheets together and smiling, looked up. A young man now occupied the place where Bethan had been sitting and she was nowhere to be seen.

Alec stood and sauntered over. As he approached him, the young man smiled and put out a waiting hand.

'Where's Bethan?'

'I dunno, she might be round here somewhere. I can take the form.'

Alec ignored the outstretched hand.

'I wanted to see Bethan.'

'Well, she might have gone to the studio. Do you want to give me the, ah —,' the young man said, and reached for the sheaf of papers and would have snatched them if Alec had not stepped smartly back.

Alec's face must have betrayed his mood, because the young man said, 'Hey, it's cool. Keep them if you want! What do I care?'

At that moment Bethan came through a door at the back of the foyer. She was wearing an old black coat, long and nipped in at the waist and a rainbow-coloured woolly hat. She was carrying a portfolio that was almost as big as she was.

'Friend of yours here,' the young man said sarcastically.

Bethan looked at Alec and gave him a puzzled frown, and then she hefted the big portfolio from one arm to the other, pinching her lips together as she did so.

'Let me,' Alec said, and barely managed to stop himself from charging her and ripping the portfolio from her hands. She gave him the case and the two left the gallery together.

When they were outside, she said, 'I'm sorry, I can't quite place you. Your name is?'

'Alec.'

'Ah,' she headed for the gate and he followed, 'so where do I know you from?'

'Well, you don't really, it's just that —,' he stopped

walking and let her go ahead through the gate. She walked a few more paces along the pavement. There was an icy wind blowing that almost took his breath away.

She stopped by a car, a pale blue Volkswagen, the old sort with the long sloping snout. She opened the door and reached for the portfolio.

'Can I give you a lift?'

'Well, I was just going home, really.'

'Hop in, where's home?'

He got into the car and sat beside her. He was still holding the questionnaire, but he'd rolled it up and was hoping she wouldn't realise what it was, because he no longer wanted her to read it.

'Okay,' she said, 'you're going to have to give me directions.'

She drove slowly. She seemed like a nervous driver: two hands on the wheel, eyes bobbing between mirror and road, stopping graciously at every pedestrian crossing.

'Okay, left here, then right at the roundabout.'

He thought how easily two people in a car, a man and a woman, felt like and would look like a couple. He imagined one of those windscreen stickers with their names on, 'Beth and Alec'. He thought about a sleek border collie lying on the back seat, its tongue lolling and mud on its paws after a long walk. Or of two children sitting back there, a boy for him and a girl for her. He even thought affectionately of the rows that they'd have; her jealousy because he'd talked too long to a beautiful woman at a party. Wouldn't it be nice to be so possessed?

'Second on the right, off this road.'

''kay.'

'And it's here on the right.

She pulled over and parked. He had to say something now. Something casual. Intelligent. Emphasizing his interest in her art. What about some lie about free tickets? Tickets to The Magic Flute? Or a new play at The Royal? Or should he try honesty?

'Oh, wow,' she said.

'I —,' he began, re-rolling and worrying the papers in his hand. He heard her open the door and get out. He opened the passenger door and walked around the car to the pavement.

The wind had dropped and it was beginning to snow.

She was standing and staring at the thing in the Neville's garden, and hugging herself.

'Wow', she said. There was no irony, 'That's brilliant. I love it and look, it's snowing!'

She lifted a palm to cup the sky and grinned.

'Yeah', he said and he imagined their dog barking wildly and trying to bite the snowflakes as they fell. And the two children whooping and cheering and throwing snowballs.

'It's my neighbours',' he said, 'I didn't like it at first,' he paused and glanced at her. She looked entranced, happy and perfect with specks of snow on her hair, her coat; one caught in a glossy black eyelash, that would melt into a tear, 'but now I kind of like it,' he said, and had the sense that he'd never before said a truer thing.

And you Read your Emily Dickinson

Some time ago a man wrote a song about a woman reading some poems that had been written by another woman who lived her whole life in almost complete isolation. Then another man, whose name was Andy, played the record of the song to his girlfriend.

This was long ago in a first-floor flat somewhere in the Uplands. There was an Indian bedspread hanging on the wall and another thrown over the settee. Dead joss sticks on the mantelpiece, white sweet-smelling ash on the tiles beneath. A candle in a bottle by the bed.

The girl, whose name was Marcie, didn't wear shoes for the whole of that summer. Maybe the year was 1976. Her feet grew hard and dirty, though her heart was as soft and sweet and delicate as an overripe strawberry.

One day, when they had been together for a week or

so, Andy had painted a delicate daisy chain around her ankle. It was done so exquisitely, so perfectly you would have thought it was real. She didn't want to wash after that. Just as sometimes after they had made love she didn't like to wash him away, but liked to feel his wetness seeping from her. Love, she thought, made all these things beautiful.

With autumn the rains came. At first the air grew hot and dry, and it seemed to hum with subdued energy. Then wind and lightening blasted themselves into being and the downpour began. The trees were stripped of their leaves overnight, it seemed.

The daisy chain had long faded from her ankle when he bought her a pair of black and white children's baseball boots from Woolworth's. They cost him seventy-five pence. For his twenty-third birthday she bought him Bob Dylan's just released 'Desire'.

They were locked in an oyster of time and all things were possible.

This is what it is to be young. It is as fleeting as a mayfly's summer, as intangible as the iridescent sheen on a dragonfly's wing.

In love, for that is what her condition was, she saw everything with an almost painfully acute clarity. The records he played for her seemed to speak directly from his soul to hers.

But then he ended it. And ended it in a crazy way. On the Monday he told her he loved her, on Tuesday he didn't ring and on Wednesday he showed up with flowers.

'This may not make sense now,' he said 'but one day

it will. I bought you these flowers as a sign of my love, but I also have something difficult that I want to say....'

Marcie had stood very still and watched Andy's face. Waited for his words. Expected him to say that he wanted to live with her or marry her or for her to have his baby.

'I think,' he said, 'I've been thinking. That is, I thought it would be best if we didn't see each other anymore.'

It took her almost fifteen years to get around to reading the Emily Dickinson poems mentioned in the song. Even though she'd always meant to.

This was when she found out about the poet's life: the years of seclusion in the upstairs room in Amherst, Massachusetts. Little Emily, she thought, with her big mournful eyes and white muslin dresses lived the life of a ghost, her poems were the ink stains of a poltergeist, fragments left over from some twilight haunting.

She had bought a slim volume of Dickinson's collected poems from a charity shop and prompted by a brief biography in the introduction she had gone to the central library in town to find out more about the poet.

She was sitting on a row of chairs behind the stacks with Volume One of a Dickinson biography on her lap when she noticed a curious, but instantly recognizable noise. It was the sound of stifled sobs. Raggedy breathing, a wet choked sound, but yet so soft and feminine. Mournful cries smothered by propriety.

Because the Emily Dickinson biography was open on her lap, for one surreal moment she imagined that the sound of weeping came from the leaves of the book. By way of experiment, she tried closing the book and the sounds did momentarily cease, but then they started again; little gasps of acute pain falling like a hesitant summer shower. She looked around for the source of the noise. On the other side of the library there was a row of four computers, which provided free internet access. Each of the machines was occupied; four people sat with their backs to her, their shoulders hunched in that familiar and busy way. From where she was she could see the kind of things they were looking at on the screens, but she could not quite read it. A bulky hulking woman in a loud floral dress was reading an email from a Hotmail account. A young man was looking at a picture of Marilyn Manson, and his sweatshirt had the word Nirvana printed above a soulful picture of Kurt Cobain.

She watched and listened for the sounds and thought 'all things pass' but did not quite know where those words had come from. Perhaps it was a line from a song, perhaps a line printed on the inside of her skin; her maker's trademark like those on a doll or an item of clothing.

Dreaming, not quite concentrating, she heard the cries again and watched the young woman with the rippling auburn hair on the far end. This girl, hair aflame and skin as white and fragile as a store-bought mushroom's, with her black boots and her black Lady Macbeth skirt and her black crocheted cardigan – a net for catching nightmares in – she must be the weeper. Yet no quiver moved her body to the rhythm of the sobs. The girl was still and calm, except for when she too was finally driven to turn her head towards the noise.

Then it was clear who the culprit was. The flesh beneath the floral print dress swelled and rippled like a breeze moving through a field of poppies.

'Oh,' the crying woman gasped, then breathed in sharply. Then again, 'Oh.'

The woman's head wobbled and faltered. It reminded Marcie of those Japanese dolls designed to warn of impending earthquakes. The woman's hair was cut very short and badly, emphasizing her solid, pink sausage neck.

Marcie wondered if someone would approach the woman to offer comfort, but no one did. Then she thought that perhaps she should do it if no one else – the librarians for example – would do it. She wondered what it was the woman had read on the screen that had upset her so. A lover's rejection? The news of a parent's death? Or that of an old friend or perhaps a much-loved pet?

Marcie remembered how on the day so many years ago when Andy had finished with her, she had pretended to go to the bathroom, deliberately leaving behind her bag and coat with a plan to sneak from the house. She had not wanted to cry in front of him, and could not cope with his words about 'staying friends' and 'being mature'. How could she manage to be in his company and yet no longer reach for him, touch his hand, his thigh, his neck? Kiss him how and whenever she liked?

She tiptoed down the stairs, watching her feet as she went, willing them to silence. Tears were welling up in her eyes and she saw her feet as an abstracted pattern of black and white, black and white flashing over the red stair carpet.

He'd clothed her feet in love. Even if it was only 75p's worth of Woolworth's love. Now he'd taken the love away and so she no longer wanted the shoes, didn't deserve them.

She sat on the bottom step and undid the laces. The boots had grown soft now and the new rubbery smell had worn off and the soles were getting thin in places.

She opened the front door and stepped out into the rain. There was a dustbin next to the porch and she lifted its silvery lid and dropped the boots in amongst the ashes and the potato peelings and the carcass of a chicken.

She set off for home. Down the hill she went, through the Uplands, a barefoot urchin with no coat, no money and no love. Tears poured down her cheeks and mixed with the rain. Her hair was plastered to her skull, her jeans grew dark and heavy and sodden. She sobbed. Her heart was breaking and yet an hour before she had been happy.

People passing stared at her. They watched from shop doorways and from under umbrellas and bus shelters. Heads turned to follow her progress as she passed pubs and cafes. No one went to her. No one offered succor. No one saw her pain as innocent or vulnerable or worth healing. She was instead freakishly mad, a wild girl on drugs. Dangerous.

She followed the road towards town, her thoughts now like a downpour, making dark puddles, mud holes of despair. She was thinking of how there was nothing for her now. That without his love the world was only rain and strangers.

But then from nowhere it seemed, there was a woman beside her hurrying to keep pace.

'Excuse me. Excuse me,' was what the woman had said.

Marcie thought she was going to ask for directions and so she stopped walking and looked at her.

The woman was middle-aged and wore a cream-coloured raincoat that flapped and blew in the wind. Under the raincoat she had on a pale blue blouse with a cameo brooch at her neck and a navy skirt. Her hair was short and styled in soft waves around her head, but very quickly it was being drenched and battered down by the rain.

'Are you alright?' the woman asked, 'can I give you a lift somewhere?'

She gestured back up the road and Marcie saw a pale blue-green Morris Minor parked haphazardly under the trees, its headlights silver beams illuminating the cascading raindrops.

Marcie hesitated, uncertain of what to do. The woman waited and Marcie saw that she was getting soaked. Her hairstyle destroyed, her expensive clothes ruined. Soon the woman would look as bedraggled and pathetic as she did and then both of them would be outcasts.

The woman reached forward and touched Marcie's shoulder. She was both tentative and tender with that touch. It was the same as when one reaches for a stray dog, uncertain if the proffered hand will be licked or bitten.

'Come on,' said the woman with more confidence now, 'I can't leave you like this.'

And that was when Marcie had flung herself at the stranger and held her like you would hold your mother and she sobbed and sobbed, and the woman made soothing noises, then led her to the car and tucked her into the passenger seat with the safety belt snuggly around her like she was being tucked up in bed.

The woman's name was Sheila Berne. She had taken Marcie to her house, told her to shower, given her enormous warm towels and a dressing gown, then homemade soup, and strong tea with whisky in.

They had sat together in the warm kitchen, rain still gusting against the windows and wind howling in the chimneys and Sheila had said, 'Now you tell me your troubles if you want to. Sometimes it helps. But if you don't want to, that's fine too.'

Marcie told her, but as she arranged the words, it all seemed so paltry and pathetic – not the end of the world at all, not a reason for choosing not to live at all, but just a bad raw hiccup, that would be forgotten in years to come.

Later, with Marcie dressed in borrowed clothes – a pretty summer frock from the fifties, tennis shoes two sizes too big, and with her wet clothes in a carrier bag, Sheila had dropped her home. As Marcie was getting out of the car, Sheila had handed her a small slip of paper.

'There's my phone number and address. If you need me, call. You don't have to be alone.'

Marcie took the piece of paper and later that evening she tucked it in between the pages of a book. She had liked the idea that Sheila would always be there for her. Would open her door and heart to Marcie's despair if ever it got that bad again. She saved up the thought of Sheila like a last chance talisman. Measured the degrees of her unhappiness by her need for Sheila. Three years went by and nothing was quite bad enough to warrant another visit.

Then one day whilst tidying her belongings Marcie came across the book that she believed held the slip of paper and fanned open the pages, but it wasn't there.

Fifteen years later it was like a dream. She saw herself back then as a girl who was so vulnerable and gullible as to be downright idiotic. Life hardens the self as rough pavements harden the soles of the feet. Few things touched her now. Maybe that was why she was here today in the library seeking out Emily Dickinson and her hard nuggets of truth and pain and beauty.

Marcie thought about standing up and pretending to look at some books on the shelf a few feet away from the crying woman. From there she could read the email, but she knew this desire was more from curiosity than concern, and that stopped her.

She kept watching, willing someone in authority to go to the woman. Wasn't it part of the librarian's duty to help people? Wasn't it more proper for them to approach than for her, a complete stranger?

Then she thought, 'Well, if no one else will, then I must,' and just as she was about to lay the Emily Dickinson book down and rise from her chair in readiness to walk the ten or so paces, the woman suddenly closed the email page, stood up and hurried out.

What Marcie felt then was an incredible relief. She had planned to be good and kind, and would have done it, but now she was released. She let out a breath and relaxed her shoulders and had the sensation that everyone else in the library was doing the same thing. The problem had picked herself up and left the building.

Marcie opened the book again and read one paragraph from the centre of the book. It satisfied and tempted her just enough to make her borrow the heavyweight two-volume work and take it home.

At the counter she handed over the plastic card with its bar code and considered mentioning the weeping woman to the librarian, but the man's brisk efficiency held her back. None of his business. None of her business. The computer system registered her presence, her loan for that day and she was done.

She left the library, negotiating the steps and the three young men who sat there smoking. She turned left in order to head for the bus, tucking the books into her bag as she went. She still felt a faint nudge of guilt scratching at the inside of her head. She knew she should have gone to the woman sooner. Then up ahead, stalled by a railing, she saw a hunched figure in a billowing tent-like dress, its splashing flowers garish against the grey town.

Fifteen, maybe twenty minutes had passed, but the weeping woman had only got this far and still she wept. Marcie slowed down, prepared herself for what she must do. This was her second chance. There was a debt to be paid and she could not balk at it, no matter how futile it was, or how unwanted or silly.

She drew level with the woman.

'Excuse me,' she said, 'excuse me, but I noticed you were upset.'

The woman turned and Marcie saw her face for the first time. It was a swollen moon face, pink and bland with unfortunate bristles on the chin. The eyes were small and colourless and showed no life.

Marcie lifted her left hand and lightly batted the woman's well-padded shoulder with the flat of her palm. She sensed the swell of flesh, hot and damp beneath the thin cotton dress. She could not quite bring herself to rest her hand there.

'Is there anything I can do? Would it help to talk?'

The woman looked away. Closed herself off again in her sorrow.

Marcie persisted, 'Are you sure?'

'No,' the woman murmured, 'no'.

'Well,' said Marcie, as she gave the shoulder one last clumsy pat, 'I'll leave you then.'

And she walked away without a backward glance; her account still partially in arrears.

And I, my Robert Frost

This was what Rachel loved (in no particular order): snow, morello cherries, Christmas carols, the smell of her own skin after a day at the beach, Jeff Buckley's *Grace* album and Gauloise cigarettes.

On their first date he'd understood that much.

'I *love* snow,' she'd said and he noticed how the word love was spoken in a lower and slower tone than the other two words.

Later, back at her shared house, she had searched for the Buckley CD. The search gave him a slice of silence in which to contemplate her as she opened CD wallets and peered in cupboards and on shelves for the elusive disk. But after fifteen minutes or so, he began to feel the CD was an excuse, that she now regretted asking him back for coffee, felt uncomfortable to find him sitting there with a friendly but expectant smile on his face.

'Hey,' he'd said, 'it doesn't matter. I don't mind what we listen to.'

'It does matter,' she had almost snapped at him. Then she let out a groan, 'Oh where is it?'

He stood, uncertain as to why he was standing; whether it was because she had been on her feet since they walked in through the door or because he was about to leave. Maybe, because he was a man, he also wanted to take control of a situation that was getting out of hand. He stepped over the wire CD rack and squatted in front of it like a supplicant in front of a stone idol. The music was surprisingly wide ranging: Queen and the Queens of the Stone Age, Abba and The Ramones, Suzanne Vega and Elvis, Velvet Underground and Charlotte Church, Townes Van Zandt and John Coltrane. But no Jeff Buckley.

He slipped the Coltrane from the rack and stood up.

'Hey, how 'bout we listen to this while we look for the other?'

She glanced with disinterest at the cover of *A Love Supreme*, then at his face. She looked as if she was torn between being polite and pleasing her guest, or ignoring him in order to carry on with her search. He suddenly felt as if he was trying to persuade the Knights of the Crusade to give up on the Holy Grail in order to watch Eastenders.

'Please,' he said, 'I haven't heard this in a while. I had the tape, but it committed hari kari in the player.'

She relented and smiling sweetly, nodded towards the ghetto blaster on the table by the window.

The room was typical of living rooms in shared houses. Sparse, but over furnished at the same time. There were two sofas and two armchairs, none of which matched, an old dining table, which someone had draped with an Indian sari, and four dining chairs, two of which were piled with newspapers. The CD player looked incongruous placed in the middle of the table; there was something both temporary and forlorn about the arrangement.

He pressed a button on the machine and the lid sprang open clumsily like a jack-in-the-box. 'Badly made,' he thought as he reached for the disc inside, and as he did, he realized that it was the CD she'd been searching for.

It seemed obvious to him, then. Obvious that this is where it would be and obvious what he should do next. He left the disk inside, gently closed the plastic top, pressed play and turned to her.

'Hey,' he said, grinning and opening his arms, 'wanna dance?'

There was a moment, a beat of time, in which she flashed her eyes at him angrily as if she was affronted by his betrayal, but then the music began. It built slowly, rising out of the silence almost imperceptibly, inscribing itself on the senses, and then suddenly soaring; sweet, plaintive and unstoppable.

'Oh,' she said, her face illuminated with pleasure, 'oh, I *love* Jeff Buckley.'

She came towards him dreamily like a sleepwalker who is moving to some secret tune in an unknown place. There was a moment of awkwardness as they drew together and negotiated arms and feet and shoulders and heads. They settled on the traditional slow dance position with her arms hooked loosely around his neck, and his around her back and a pocket of hesitant air between their bodies. They swayed together like two stalks subjected to the same elemental forces.

Later, she led him by the hand up the stairs to her room in the attic.

That is to say, she held him in one hand and Jeff Buckley in the other. When they made love it seemed there were three of them in on the act and he was uncertain if her ecstasy was the product of his physical efforts or Jeff's musical and spiritual ones.

What kind of man, he wondered much later, is threatened by snow and morello cherries and sun-baked skin and a musician called Jeff Buckley? A man who is uncertain of his significance, a dark inner demon answered, a sorry man, a weak man. Later still, when in love with a different woman, he saw that the uncertainty and jealousy and raw-edged anxiety were not symptoms of full-blown passionate love, but the reaction to his attachment to a contrary and dishonest girl, who gave with one hand and robbed him of his sanity with the other.

'You look a little like him, you know,' she had said in the morning.

'Mm hmm...,' he'd replied, hardly registering her words, perhaps because his mind had given itself over entirely to the visual. Maybe this was at the heart of desire; the drowning out of logic in the flood of seeing; her clear skin still washed with gold from the long hot summer, her eyes bright and shining, the brown irises flecked with yellow. Her mouth, not perfect, but shapely and quirky, hiding crooked teeth.

At that moment, in the sinful morning after, she had propped herself up on one elbow and traced a delicate finger over his face while the covers had slipped to caress her ribs. He had sleepily skimmed his eyes over her body, met her eyes then, returned to her breasts. Then again, he shifted his gaze, confronting her eyes, then her two brown nipples. His eyes flicked between them. There were each paired magnets drawing him. Nipples like the two phony eyes on a butterfly's wings.

The physiology of desire. He was a man, an animal hard wired to respond to this. He was a slave to old patterns of reproduction. He was helpless.

And deaf.

Only after did he remember what she said. 'You look like him, you know.'

'Mm hmm.'

'You don't know who I'm talking about, do you?'

'Huh?'

He reached for her breast, weighed it in his hand, strummed a thumb over her nipple.

'Hey?' she said.

'Shut up,' he said and made her shut up by gently silencing her mouth with his.

By the end of the month he'd moved in with her.

The lease was up on his place. In the summer, his home – a room above a boathouse with a view over the lake – was too valuable to be let to a student for a student's meagre rent. And Rachel had said, 'Move here, stay with me. Be with me. We can be together.'

And so he moved in with her. Because it made sense. Or seemed to then.

After that, during all the various stages of 'later' and 'later still', with their implied and accumulated experience and maturity, he began to see that it had been a terrible mistake. A hiccup in an otherwise calm life.

But it had seemed the easy thing to do at the time. And moving in was hardly complicated as he didn't own much back then. Not enough to fill the car, or even the boot. All he owned was piled on the back seat. A radio, a duvet, a pillow, two clean sheets, a holdall stuffed with clothes, three cardboard boxes of books, an alarm clock, a toothbrush, a razor, a comb, two tins of beans, one tube of tomato paste, a chipped mug, a clutch of pens and pencils, a carrier bag of cassette tapes and nothing to play them on. He'd thrown away the cassette player when it ate up one too many of his favourite tapes. Coltrane had been the last straw.

She'd helped him carry everything to her room in the attic and then she'd gone down to the first floor for a bath.

She had a bookshelf in the room, but only four books. One shelf was filled with a row of ornaments: an old rag doll, china figurines of cats and dogs and frogs and elephants, a trinket box decorated with garlands of pink roses, all spaced out to fill the emptiness. He carefully moved them all to one end, so that they crowded together like people waiting for a train. In the space he'd made he put three piles of books.

When she came back, wrapped in a towel, damp and shining and sweet smelling from the bath, she had noticed what he had done straight away.

'Oh,' she said, 'you've moved things.'

'Well, yeah.'

'But they don't look nice like that.'

'Oh, sorry,' he'd said, 'I was just, you know, unpacking. I can put them back if...'

'No, no. It's okay.'

Those were the words that came out of her mouth, but her face told a different story.

'You've got a lot of books,' she'd said that evening.

'No,' he said, 'that's nothing.'

She got up and moved to the bookcase and plucked one at random.

He saw the book she'd chosen and went and took it from her.

'Sit,' he'd ordered, 'I'll read it to you.'

She sat.

'Stopping by Woods on a Snowy Evening,' he read.

'Oh, I love snow,' she said.

'Ssh,' he said, then, '*whose woods these are I think I know, His house is in the village though...*'

She listened as he read the poem. He found himself rocking on his heels as he recited the last two lines, the repeated phrase, '*And miles to go before I sleep.*'

When he was done, he smiled at her and clapped the book shut.

'Is that the end?'

'Yes, did you like it?'

'Where's he going?'

'Well, you don't need to know that.'

'I thought the bloke whose woods they were was going to come and like, shoot him or something.'

'Um, well, yes, there is an atmosphere of menace. But it's about mood and mystery.'

'But where's he going?'

'It doesn't matter.'

'Yeah, it does. Why does he have to travel all night in the snow?'

'I don't know.'

She clucked her tongue on the roof of her mouth and looked cheated.

'Rachel,' he'd said, 'didn't you like it?'

She wrinkled her nose.

'I thought you'd like it.'

He flopped beside her on the bed, then sighed and held the book across his chest.

She got up and – businesslike – began to rub her hair with the towel. Dressed herself, then sat on the edge of the bed and put her hair in two long braids. Fastened the ends with elastic bands.

'What do you think?' she said when she was done. She offered him herself for his inspection. Her face had the scrubbed gleam of newly-washed skin and that, together with the braids, made her look as if she were just fourteen years old.

'Cute,' he'd said without enthusiasm.

He didn't like her housemates and they didn't seem to like either her or him. He found himself thinking of his old room above the boathouse. The sounds of water lapping, the birdsong at dawn, the lovely spartan bleakness of it. The bare floorboards and thin moth-eaten curtains. He even began to think affectionately of the cold there through the long winter, which seemed now to have been invigorating rather than punishing.

Jeff, his landlord, had said he could return in mid September, but he hadn't given that a second thought.

One Sunday towards the end of August, when Rachel was working at the hotel, he drove out to the lake. He parked on the road just beyond the house and followed the public footpath that skirted it. The house seemed empty, but an unfamiliar car was parked around the back and in it he glimpsed a child's booster seat and noticed that the back windows were smeared with little dirty handprints.

He sat at the side of the lake and surveyed all that he thought of as his. In his jacket pocket he'd brought the Robert Frost book and now he took it and turned to the poem he'd read to Rachel.

He read it through twice. He still didn't quite know why he liked it so much; maybe it was because he saw himself at the edge of the woods and felt the urgency of those 'promises to keep' and 'the miles to go'.

At the back of the book there were three blank pages, and without more than a moment's consideration, he tore one of them out and scribbled a hasty note to Jeff, which he posted through the letterbox in the boathouse.

Rachel had worked a double shift that day, and came home grumpy and smelling of chip fat. She put her tips in the big whiskey bottle she kept in the wardrobe and they rattled like chains as they fell.

'Rachel,' he'd started to say, 'Rachel, you know how I'll be moving out in a couple of weeks, well...'

'What?' she'd said.

'Well, to make it fair I'll...'

'What? What are you on about?'

He didn't know why he was about to lie so blatantly except he felt there was something bigger and stronger out there, and it was calling him.

'Well, you know this was only temporary. That the boathouse would be va...'

'I knew? What do you mean "I knew"? We're living together. We're a couple, we....'

She stopped then and covered her face with her hands, stifling a sob. He stepped closer and for that solitary moment he was on the brink of asking her to come to the boathouse to live with him.

'Rachel,' he said, 'Would you...'

Something hit him hard in the face and took his words away. One of her shoes, a black, low-heeled Mary Jane, fell near his feet. 'Christ,' he said, and looked at her. She was taking off the other shoe and screwing up her eyes, preparing to take aim.

He ducked by the side of the wardrobe and the second shoe clattered against the mirror on its door.

'You fucker,' she shouted, 'you bloody lying bastard!' and more things bounced around the room. A hairbrush, a carton of talcum powder. A telephone directory, a cushion. He danced and ducked across the room, narrowly escaping the missiles including a heavy crystal glass elephant that smashed into the wall just as he reached the door.

'Rachel; I promised Jeff I'd go back.'

'You liar,' she screamed and reached for another ornament.

'I promised.'

He had always thought there was something noble about a promise. A man of honour kept to his solemn oaths no matter what. Even if you had to ride all night in the snow, the promise must be fulfilled.

'I have promises to keep,' he told himself as he made his way downstairs.

He got to his car and opened the door, sat behind the wheel with an overwhelming sense of relief. He didn't quite know where he was going but it didn't matter. He said the poem's last line again, *and miles to go before I sleep,* and put the key in the ignition. Snow would have been nice and also horse to ride, but the car would do and it was at least, getting dark. His promise was as phony as hell but maybe that didn't matter, he'd make good on it soon enough.

As he drove back towards the lake he thought about how some things just can't be explained; like why snow is beautiful or why a poem moves us, or even why we lie, and how it was sometimes better that way – the secrets kept, the promises broken.

Home

The mother-in-law's car is white; a long estate with a cage at the back where the dogs can travel. It smells a bit doggy in there still, even though the two golden retrievers have been in the kennels for a fortnight and the car has been valeted and scrubbed and sprayed and disinfected.

The car is travelling along the West Way, heading into the setting sun. The sky is putting on a magnificent show, an hallucinogenic vision of scarlet and purple and tangerine; not that anyone much appreciates it. London slips away beneath them; factories, looming blocks of council flats, red brick houses rosy in the evening light. Then the buildings become sparser and there are the beginnings of fields and the air becomes cooler and fresher and the night darker.

The mother-in-law drives and the daughter-in-law sits in the back seat, her husband in the front.

The mother and son chat and he puts cassettes in the player and turns up the volume. She can't hear what they're talking about up front. For a while she sits up on the edge of her seat with one hand draped over his shoulder. He holds her hand for about a minute, and then he lets go in order to riffle through the tapes.

It doesn't seem to bother them that she isn't joining in the conversation, so she sits back and for a while, from the outskirts of London to Reading, she gazes through the window and watches the mist soften the landscape and mute its sharp greens into something more delicate.

Her mother-in-law, who decreed that Nicky couldn't travel by public transport in her condition, had insisted on this journey. Nicky is eight months' pregnant and it's the hottest May for seventy years.

They are taking her 'home'. Home is down the M4 to Cardiff. She thinks of the motorway as an umbilical cord which links mother London to the child, Wales. Or perhaps it's the other way around, she can't decide.

She no longer thinks of Wales as home. Home is Shepherds Bush. Or more particularly, the ground floor flat with the security bars on the window and the pink elephant wallpaper in the box room that will soon be the nursery.

She put the wallpaper up while he was at work and the crib was supposed to be delivered the same day, but it never arrived. When he came in from work she was in the nursery crying. He asked her what was wrong and she couldn't explain. That was three days ago and now they were taking her home. Home to see her Mum, Dad, three brothers and two Grans. Home for a 'bit of a rest'. But visiting family and eating cake and smiling will wear her out. The two Grans have already begun to send her things for the baby; white and lemon knitted bootees, which are elaborate and unusable relics from the age before the Babygro.

Those tiny woollen shoes make her think about the baby inside her, its little feet clothed only in amniotic fluid and flesh. She thinks how raw the world must feel to the newborn, the air itself scratching like nylon lace.

After they have passed the outskirts of Slough, she lays down on the seat with her head on a folded cardigan that smells of Chanel perfume. She has seen the bottle that the scent came in; the mother-in-law keeps it on a shelf in the bathroom.

The first time he took her to his mother's house, she had not been afraid, she felt at ease with herself, with him, with her. The world felt light and airy. She had a sense that everything was right and natural, like a finger dipped in a tumbler of tepid water; there were no edges or differences to be felt.

Since the pregnancy however, she has felt increasingly uncomfortable when she is with the two of them.

The baby was a kind of, sort of, lustful accident – as much his fault as hers. 'Sod it,' he'd said when she had tried to wriggle out of his arms and head for the bathroom where she kept her diaphragm.

'But Max,' she'd said, 'I might...'

'I don't care,' he'd said and they did it on the floor in

the hall with that hard, sharp, dirty hunger that sometimes still overtook them.

What did it mean when he said he didn't care? She has often remembered that and wondered about it. At first she had understood it as meaning he cared about nothing but her, and if she fell pregnant, then that was fate and he would be happy about it. But lately she has been troubled by the creeping idea that it actually meant that he cared for nothing beyond that moment.

She had talked about starting a family, but he'd always put it off in such a way that he'd made it seem that he was being responsible. No baby until they'd moved to a proper house, or until he'd got the promotion he wanted. No baby when they still dreamed of taking a year out to travel and pursue dreams and finally shed their irresponsible selves. No baby until they were grown up.

She was twenty-seven and he was eleven years older, but at weekends they'd still do crazy things like taking E and dancing half the night. Or they did until the baby.

Last night they'd stayed in together and he'd dug out his old albums from the eighties, Talking Heads and Elvis Costello and Squeeze. He played Up the Junction twice and turned up the volume and sang along.

I never thought it would happen with me and a girl from Clapham, out on the windy common, that night I have forgotten.

He also sang along to Psycho Killer and Watching the Detectives. He looked angry as he sang, but he was just aping the style of the vocalists. Rattling the cage of his lost youth, trying to get back in.

Amongst his most prized possessions was a book about punk; mostly because he was in one of the photos. It showed him pogo-ing with the crowds at the hall in West Runton. In the picture his mouth was agape as if he were screaming and it looked like he was dripping with sweat, but actually someone had tipped a pint over him moments before.

She had been eight or nine when that photo was taken; she'd probably been tucked up in bed reading *Charlie and the Chocolate Factory*. She would never be as old as him, although she felt that she was growing older by the second. Despite her doubts, lying there on the back seat of the car, she began to feel sleepy and safe. Lights from the motorway poured in, over and around her, yellow-grey. Every so often white headlights illuminated the interior and traced a journey through the car, over the seats, the roof, and the heads of the car's occupants.

The sky was now a pale wash of cloud, and trees passed; black complications of scribble at the edge of her vision. She saw the odd electricity pylon loom up with geometric certainty like an alien god. The moon looked cold and distant. Lonely even.

She slept.

The mother and son in the front were making small talk and every so often the mother had looked in the rear view mirror to see how her daughter-in-law was doing. When she saw that the girl was lying down, and noted the big belly rising and falling in slow sleepy pulses, she said, 'Nicky? Are you asleep?'

The younger woman didn't answer. Her husband twisted himself around in his seat to look at her.

'She's asleep,' he says, and he and his mother seem to relax. He turns down the volume on the cassette a little and for a while neither of them speaks.

Then the mother says 'So. How are things?'

The son replies by glancing again at the figure reclining on the back seat and lifts his two hands in a gesture of helplessness.

The mother purses her lips and says, 'Give me one of those mints, will you?'

Obediently he rummages around in the pocket on the passenger's side door, finds a yellow buttermint, unwraps it and pops it into his mother's mouth for her.

Such acts of familiarity and intimacy have existed between the mother and her son since he was seven, which was when his father died in a freak accident in 1968.

There are no apron strings tying him to his mother; he is a free man and she, with her many lovers is equally free. She had passed on to her son the philosophy of life by which she increasingly sustained herself.

There is a blackboard in the kitchen of his mother's house, which is meant for chalking up shopping lists and other reminders, but at the top, carefully spelled out in permanent white paint is the motto by which she lives her life:

Nothing can be kept – except the moment.

He grew up on shadows. A lost father, a wandering mother, the watered down ideas of Sartre, de Beauvoir, Camus, Freud, and R D Laing.

Clever ghosts, smart-ass 'uncles', poseurs, sycophants, suave, footloose bon viveurs after a fast buck. Yet, he did seek permanence for himself. The fixed steady place where he imagined he would someday somehow settle.

But now he had made a mistake. He had forged a bond of flesh more permanent than marriage. It was hard to imagine that his wife's great swollen belly contained his son or daughter. No matter how much he read about pregnancy, despite all the miracle pictures he'd seen of the inside of the womb, he could not quite believe that his wife was anything but fat. It was as if she had gorged on rich food for week after week, had stuffed herself with cakes and creamy sauces and pasta and buttery potatoes until her stomach had swelled and she groaned with the discomfort of it.

He was angry with her. Felt that he too would be consumed; gobbled up by that beautiful mouth of hers. Her teeth were small and sharp; a piranha's. Her tongue, rough as a kitten's would lick his bones clean.

He knew this was all madness; that his anger was in reality for himself. He knew that she was blithe and innocent and happy, but that didn't help, it just made him angrier.

'I suppose she must get homesick.'

His mother's voice shakes him from his reverie.

'Hmmm?'

'London is a hard place.'

'Oh, yeah.'

'If you're not used to it.'

'I guess.'

'Has she mentioned moving back?'

'Well, we talked about it. You know, if we sold the flat we could buy a pretty big place in Cardiff and still have fifty thousand or so to play with.'

The mother turns quickly to see her son's face, then she looks back at the road. His expression, so far as she could make out in that snapshot glance, was blank.

'But what about your work? Your job? The firm doesn't have a Cardiff office, does it?'

'No.'

'So, what? You'd resign?'

'I dunno. I guess I could commute...'

'Well, that's insane. You'd be exhausted. Better to keep the flat and get a little place down there for weekends.'

'Hmmm.'

'Listen. I could help with the money for that.'

'Well, that's nice, but I don't see the point.'

'What do you mean "you don't see the point"?'

'Well, what do I want with weekends down there?'

'You'll want to see the baby won't you?'

'Well... oh, I see. You mean Nicky and the baby would...'

'Yes, and then you'd see them on the weekends.'

'Right.'

'And everyone would be happy.'

Once the word 'happy' has been said, they lapse into silence.

He is thinking about that last word. Is anyone ever happy? He used to be happy at Christmastime when he was kid, but was that happiness or just greed? He used to be happy when he found bargains in junk shops. He found a really cool 1950's suede jacket in a skip once. It was his size and in almost perfect nick. Wearing that jacket he'd felt not only cool, but also clever for spotting it and also lucky because he'd got there at the right time.

Now he could walk into a shop in Soho or on the King's Road and buy almost anything he wanted and he did just that pretty often, but it never made him feel happy.

He didn't really believe Nicky and the baby living in Cardiff would make anyone happier, but he let the words settle on the three of them like silent and invisible snow.

The mother-in-law concentrated on her driving. She didn't much like motorways; they were too hypnotic, too steady and grey and relentless. She preferred variety, a challenge.

She distracted herself as she drove by doing mathematical sums in her head and trying to guess how much a little terraced house in a cheap part of Cardiff might cost. Sixty thousand? Seventy thousand? Eighty? When she thought about it costing as much as eighty she considered the idea of it as an investment. Keeping it in her name. Then she thought that if it were in her name she'd be liable for its upkeep and so on, so maybe she ought to charge rent.

He couldn't pay rent, he had enough on his hands with the mortgage on the London flat, but if they separated? Well, there was the dole, wasn't there?

The car passed the turn-off for Swindon, then Bristol. It was fully dark as they neared the Severn Bridge services. They had agreed earlier to stop here for a quick coffee, so the older woman steered into the correct lane and followed the looping road around to the car park.

Nicky woke up when the car came to a standstill. She sat up, still groggy with sleep, and yawned, stretching. The baby moved inside, performing a watery flutter; pressing a foot or hand hard against her ribs as if it were a swimmer pushing off from the side of a swimming pool.

A couple of months back, when the baby's first movements were still new and exciting, she had asked her mother-in-law if she wanted to feel the little kicks and ripples. Everyone had laid their hands on her life-filled belly; her husband first, then all her friends and all the girls at work, then the manageress and even the man at the garage. People loved to share in that secret life beneath her skin, to thrill in each quiver, each little mute hello.

They had been invited to Sunday lunch at his family's Chelsea Mews. His mother's current partner, George, was there and he had been lumbered with the cooking. He had that beaten look about him. He was wearing her flowered apron, and his walrus moustache seemed to make him look even more miserable. Though maybe he was happy enough, as Max's mother was still an attractive woman in a *Country Living* sort of way.

Nicky was sitting next to her mother-in-law on the couch when she felt the baby's movement begin.

'Oh' she'd said, and she'd put her hands over her belly, 'it's moving.'

Max had laid a hand on her stomach, and smiled. There was such love between them then, such a sense of hope and rightness.

She turned to her mother-in-law and kind of tilted her body towards her, offering herself.

'The baby's moving,' she said, 'do you want to feel it?'

The mother-in-law frowned at her as if she were an imbecile. Then she rose from the couch, and went to the drinks' cabinet. Her back was turned. She poured herself a whisky, took a sip and then, without looking at Nicky, she said, 'It loses its novelty after a while, you know,' and she turned and smiled, but the smile could not wipe her words away.

Nicky tried to forget it; she thought she was being oversensitive. Maybe it was just hormones.

The three of them got out of the car and began walking towards the service station; beyond it the bridge was arcing gracefully across the estuary to Wales.

The mother-in-law put her arm around Nicky's shoulder as they walked. She raised her other hand and swept it expansively towards the bridge and the country beyond it.

'There,' she said, as if bestowing a great gift, 'almost home.'

She squeezed Nicky's shoulder, 'Almost home.'

Sad Girl

My father told me that when he first saw my mother, he thought she looked like the saddest girl he ever saw.

He was a grill chef and she was the new waitress. They worked in the King's Hotel in Tenby, except it wasn't a hotel, not in the way you'd expect; there were no bedrooms, no overnight guests, just a bar downstairs and a restaurant upstairs.

'Saddest girl I ever saw,' was what he said. It was what he always said about my mother and then he'd get sad too, and so I'd go and put my arms around his neck and kiss him.

She had died in a traffic accident not long after I'd been born, and I'd been with her too, in a Moses basket on the back seat of the car and in the papers they'd called me 'the miracle baby'. But dad said that, in his view, miracle babies were the ones whose mothers didn't die tragically young.

Because I never knew her, everything he said about my mother had a sort of fairytale poignancy. It affected me it was in the same way that a story that began 'long ago in a land faraway...' affected me, and the sadness he spoke of seemed to suggest a sort of foretelling of her eventual fate. We lived with the ghost of my mother in a way that Grandma thought was very wrong. But when a child is raised alongside ghosts she will not be much bothered. Knowing no different, she will accept her life as a poor child will accept, and even relish, bread and dripping.

My mother's ghost had many forms. She was words, 'the saddest girl I ever saw', and she was whispers after twilight, 'John, she's not coming back, you have to start living.' She was a whole wardrobe full of clothes; a pink bobbly Chanel suit, a long chiffon dress with an aquamarine pattern of swirls and curls, a crisp white tennis dress and navy bell bottoms. She was a dressing table set of hair brush, mirror and clothes brush. She was scarlet nail varnish dried hard in the little glass bottle. She was in the favourite green vase that *must* sit on the table in the hall and could not be moved.

Grandma would sometimes threaten us that one day she'd come and take away all my mother's things, but she never did. Eventually she seemed to give up on the idea of stealing away my mother's ghost and she left us in peace for a long time. She lived on the other side of town in a big pink villa, which had been in the family since my great-great-great grandfather built it in 1802.

I suppose she tried to be a mother to me in some ways, buying me presents of frothy and fraudulently girly-pink dresses, then hinting about a coming time when I'd appreciate her, which I guessed would be the time when I'd sprout breasts and all that. Despite this, a distance remained between us that couldn't be bridged, and I'm still not sure whose fault that was: hers or mine? My father's, or my poor sad long dead mother's?

At thirteen, I was a slight pale girl who still showed no sign of sprouting breasts, and I had given up on the idea that my dad might ever get married again. Thankfully, I had stopped reading all of those fairy stories with their cruel stepmothers who might put frogs on my tongue to make me ugly, or give me strychnine-laced apples. As far as I was concerned Dad and me were all we ever wanted or needed. Though of course, this didn't stop me from thinking that one day a prince would come thrashing through the nettles and thorns of my life and sweep me off to happy ever after, mercilessly dumping dad along the way.

At about that time Grandma called around unexpectedly one Saturday evening. Dad and I were about to watch *The Generation Game*, which we dreamed about being contestants on as soon as I turned 16. We glanced at each other at the sound of the doorbell and he raised his eyes to heaven, which was something I loved to see him do, because he only ever did it in a comical, exaggerated way.

We went to the door together, even racing each other somewhat, and we swung the door open, both of us laughing and smiling, to find Grandma – accompanied by a woman I had never seen before.

'John, Elizabeth, darlings, I hope I haven't caught you on the hop?' Grandma swept into the house as she spoke, not waiting to be asked, and the woman followed.

Grandma led the way into the living room and we all trailed in her wake.

Bruce Forsyth was saying 'Nice to see you, to see you...' and the audience chorused 'nice!' Then Grandma pressed the button on the TV and the screen went blank.

There was a moment when we all stood around in the sudden silence as if each of us was waiting for the next thing to happen, whatever that might be.

'Well,' my father said and he clapped his hands together in a hopeful way.

Grandma took charge. She had a habit of doing that, of taking over, of acting like this was her home and we were the guests.

'Sit down, sit down,' she ordered, and when we were seated she said, 'now who's for tea?'

She whisked from the room, which left the three of us: myself, Dad and the strange woman, all sitting rather awkwardly as we each tried to arrange ourselves into relaxed poses.

My father had a searching look on his face as if he was thinking very hard of what to say.

'We were about to watch *The Generation Game*,' he informed Grandma's friend as if it weren't obvious.

The woman glanced up very quickly, sneaked a look at my father, muttered Oh, and took to inspecting her hands.

She was a big woman, not only tall but also with big bosoms and big legs and big hands. Even her hair was big, very dark and long and bushy and kinky and it sat over her shoulders like a bearskin cape.

I took the opportunity to take a good look at her, though you could barely see her face under all that hair, but I noticed other things. She had on pink nail varnish, which was a little chipped and her nails were chewed down which made her hands look rather chunky. She wore black court shoes with low heels, and they looked old and worn and you could see how over time her toes had pushed themselves into the leather, leaving their lumpy impression. Around her neck she wore a simple gold cross on a chain and when I saw that I thought, 'Uh-oh...'

Grandma came in then and started fussing with the nest of tables. My father helped and pretty soon there were two tables standing in front of the settee and they'd been laid with embroidered cloths and those dainty little pastry forks we never used, and the cups and saucers with the rosebud pattern.

Grandma came back and forward from the kitchen. She was wearing the apron that she always kept in our kitchen that had a pattern of big red splashy flowers; peonies or dog roses, but she still had on her hat, which was a pale blue silk turban to match her pale blue blouse. She brought in the teapot, the jug of milk, two plates of sandwiches and the tiered china cake stand that I don't think I'd ever seen in use before. Arranged on it were French fancies, jam tarts, butterfly cakes and wedges of cherry sponge.

Dad and I knew that she had brought all of this food with her, but we also knew we shouldn't say anything about that; we should just smile and tuck in and try not to embarrass her.

In all the fuss my grandmother never actually introduced us to the woman, but we got to know her name soon enough.

'Sally-Anne is teaching Sunday school at St Jude's. Sally-Anne went to the teacher's training college, but never got a chance to work at teaching. Sally-Anne's mother was disabled, she had to nurse her, didn't you dear?'

When asked a direct question, the woman would peek out from behind her hair and mumble, 'Yes,' 'No,' or 'Mmm.'

Grandma did most of the talking, either telling us things we didn't want to know about Sally-Anne, or telling Sally-Anne stuff about us that we didn't want told.

'Elizabeth came third in the Eisteddfod for her poem. Elizabeth was such a good baby, her very first word was Grandma, you know.'

This wasn't strictly true, Dad had told me my first word was 'Da-da' but as he'd failed to report this to Grandma at the time, he'd let her bask in the lie all these years. Grandma had lost her husband and her only daughter, and I suppose I was meant to be some sort of consolation prize.

'John was a top chef. Cordon bleu, you know, but he had to give that up. Unsociable hours, you know. But now he's a top clerical officer.'

'Well,' my father said, 'I don't know about "top", but...'

There was a lull in the conversation as my father's voice trailed off. Sally-Anne slowly raised her hand.

'Yes, dear,' Grandma said, and we all turned to look at Sally-Anne because it seemed that at last she was going to join in the conversation. She blushed and stammered, 'Could I please... I need the ah... ladies room.'

Grandma led her out and directed her up the stairs. Dad looked at me and smiled and rolled his eyes.

Grandma began clearing the tea things away and we both automatically stood up and helped her. We'd nearly finished clearing up, when from upstairs we heard the mechanism on the toilet rattle, but no flush. The toilet was temperamental, there was a knack to getting it to work, which we'd all learned and took for granted. It rattled again twice, but still there was no roar of gushing water.

'Oh dear' said Dad.

Grandma, catching on, went and stood at the bottom of the stairs and bellowed up, 'Wait a minute, lift the handle, then pull down sharply.'

We hovered about in the hall, all of us with our ears tuned to the tricky operation going on upstairs. A minute passed and we heard the same useless ratcheting noise.

Grandma called up with further instructions. I imagined Sally-Anne trapped in that tiny room, a great big woman unable to leave until she'd managed to make the stubborn mechanism work, and it struck me as really comical. A smirk must have started creeping onto my face, because my dad nudged me hard in the ribs.

'Oh dear,' said Grandma, 'you'd better go up and help,' and she was looking at me.

'Me?' I said.

'Well, your father can't go, can he?'

'Oh.'

I didn't see why Grandma couldn't go as it was her friend, but then Grandma would have thought it was all a bit undignified; not a lady's job at all.

I started up the stairs and my grandmother was scolding my father for not getting the plumbing fixed years ago.

I stood by the toilet door and called Hello, but Sally-Anne's only answer was more hollow metallic rattling. I knocked on the door, and I could hear her shuffling around inside and her heels clumping about on the lino.

Although I found the whole situation funny I also felt a bit sorry for this strange lady and so I pretended that I wasn't there to rescue her, but because I needed the toilet.

'I want to go,' I said, 'it's urgent.'

There was a mutter, then more clumping feet, and one more useless attempt at the flush before she finally unbolted the door with a loud click and I stepped aside to let her pass. I was trying to be friendly and casual, and so I looked her right in the eyes and gave her what I thought was my brightest, most beguiling smile.

It was only then that I saw her face properly, as she had suddenly and indignantly, lifted up her chin, which made her hair fall back from her face. Her lips were set in a harsh fleshless sneer and her cheeks had high vivid spots of colour. Standing so close, I got a real sense of her height, and I felt tiny, like some little mouse that was cornered by a big angry bear.

It was her eyes that really got to me, there seemed to be no colour in the irises, only a black shining gleam. They fixed on me and I had the sensation that I was about to be eaten.

But then we sort of sidestepped around each other in an awkward square dance – the landing was small and had a few bits of overflow furniture, a chest of drawers and a small cupboard. She paused for a moment and straightened her skirt. I lingered by the open door to the toilet, feeling I should try to say sorry, though I didn't really know what for.

After she had finished fussing with her skirt, she turned and gave me one last look of withering hatred, then in some perverse attempt at personal grooming, she slipped both hands under her hair and flicked it up violently. It brushed my chin and mouth in a great waft of fuzzy Vosene. It seemed a gesture of both violence and intimacy, and I couldn't make sense of it. I wished at that moment that my mother were still alive; I thought that perhaps only a mother could explain all the dark secrets of womanhood, that only she could protect me.

I lingered upstairs after I had flushed the toilet. I washed my hands in the sink and gazed at myself in the small mirror on the bathroom cabinet. I glowered, trying to make my eyes black with fury like hers had been, but I just looked like me; a child with pale clear skin and freckles, and a silly scowl.

After they had made their departure; Sally-Anne murmuring Bye-bye, with her head held low and sheepish once more, my grandmother gushing and fussing and kissing and looking very pleased with herself, my father sat on the armchair and smiled to himself.

I got the *Radio Times* and flicked through to Saturday, *Some Like it Hot* was due on in ten minutes.

'Dad,' I said 'Dad, can we watch this film? It's got Marilyn Monroe and Tony Curtis.'

He was still grinning to himself and murmured, distractedly, 'Hmm?'

I told him again about the film. I was desperate to recover the moments before Grandma had come, to replace our lost-forever episode of The Generation Game with something equally right and good for a girl and her dad on a Saturday night.

'Yes, yes,' he said 'whatever you want, sweetheart,' then in a dreamy way he turned and looked me in the eye. 'That Sally-Anne,' he said, 'didn't she look sad? Did you ever see anyone who looked as sad as that?'

I said No and my voice had this hard edge to it and I think I might have scowled; my eyes burning bright and hard, but he didn't see, he had already turned away.

Circle Games

I

He was born in Tepee Valley, east of Aberystwyth, a handful of miles from the coast. When he was two, his mother and some other people squatted a deserted farmhouse within walking distance of the tepees and their house became the commune's unofficial base and washroom.

His mother called him Ethan. Until he was nine years old, he did not exist, which is to say that as far as the world of bureaucracy and census were concerned, he did not exist. There was no medical record of his birth; no certificate and no National Insurance number laying in wait for him in the future like a trap that snares a rabbit. He was as free as a bird.

When he was around seven or eight, he noticed Lisa, one of his mother's friends taking a small tablet.

'What's that?' he asked.

Lisa told him it was Valium. He asked what it was for. But no one would answer him. Later, when Lisa had gone upstairs, his mother told him that she was very sad because of the way the world was, because of wars and starving children and old women who had to work in the fields until they dropped dead from tiredness. 'And Hiroshima,' she'd said, 'and Treblinka, and My Lai...'

'Oh,' he'd said, understanding only that some special wisdom had been passed onto him.

He thought for a little while. People came and went in the communal kitchen around him. He poured some of the brown sugar onto the table and pushed it around, making mountains and valleys and streams. Then he squashed and scattered them, wondering how it must feel to be a god.

'Does the tablet make it go away?' he asked at last.

'Make what go away?' his mother asked.

'All the wars and death and that.'

Ant answered him, 'Does Valium make wars stop? Make starvation stop? Yeah, it's like magic. Puff! They're gone just like that!' Ant waved his hands in the air like a magician and rolled his eyes to show how everything was easily fixed.

'Really?' asked Ethan.

'Yep.'

'Really and truly?'

'Yeah,' Ant said and he drew the word out long and

slow, and added this hint of something that was sarcasm, but Ethan missed it.

'Wow,' he said, 'cool.'

He remembered that moment in its totality. It was one of those memories preserved in amber, where he recalled everything; from the faces of the people gazing at him, to the particular position of furniture and windows, the smells and sounds, and lastly and most surprisingly, even a sense of his own almost weightless, and yet awkward child's body.

In his mind's eye he could still see the way that his mother's hair was frayed at the edges (that was how he thought of it then) instead of being smooth and softly curling. He saw the way her breasts moved under her loose clothes; how they swung or lifted as she raised her arm to pour tea or knead dough. He saw her naked feet were almost as black with dirt as his own. He smelled her smells; apple shampoo, cigarette breath and that other stuff, musk oil. And that day she'd been crushing garlic for the casserole, and when she reached for his face and lifted him by his chin to smile at him, her fingers had smelled of it.

He remembered the way the sunlight had fallen through the smeared window, dappled and gently moving as the trees outside swayed slowly in a breeze. He could picture Ant's face; his long chin and longer forehead, and the stubbornly long strands of greasy black hair that fell over his shoulders and down his back. He could see the crumbs on the wooden breadboard, and the places where the knife had scored shallow lines on it. And on the window ledge, a jam-jar with a pierced top; inside of which was some sugary water, dead wasps, and one which was still angrily, noisily living.

He saw Alan's yellow fingers and the way he cupped a cigarette so that the smoke snaked up and over his hand. He heard the dog sigh plaintively as it settled down to sleep on the flagstones under the table. He smelled the sweet perfume of cut grass wafting through the open door. Saw Jessie cutting the weeds in the front garden and heard the almost imperceptible sounds of the hand scythe as it chopped through the thick stems.

Remembering always made an idyll of everything, even the unpleasant bits. Remembering gave him a pang of hurt at something unnamed that was lost even then.

And why remember that day of all days? Why these particular minutes of time? He should have remembered other things; being evicted and leaving the house in the country, the last time he saw his father, his mother's illness. He should have remembered the shock of the new flat; the surprise of the city, the smells of school, and the unfamiliar rub of a nylon shirt at his neck.

He knows the facts of his life of course, but that's not the same as remembering, and there are years which are vague and out of focus. In his next real memory he's suddenly twelve or thirteen, and he's lying on his bed in the new flat, which is in an ugly concrete tower block off Carmarthen Road in Swansea. It is summer and the sun is sinking, and the sky is red and it lights the room with its colours, and he is bored. So bored he could die. He can feel all the evenings of his life stretching out like this, endless and empty, and irritation is boiling up in him because he feels so bloody useless. And it occurs to him that nothing is going to change. That this is it. This is going to be how it is until he dies. And so what's the point? And then he imagines holding a gun in his hand.

His brain is working overtime, because as he lies there with his hand resting on the coverlet palm up, he begins to really feel the gun there. He doesn't look at his hand because that would spoil it. But it's there sure enough, and his forefinger is lightly touching the trigger. He tightens his grasp around the handgrip, teases his finger on the trigger and then slowly he lifts the gun to his head. He puts the muzzle against his right temple; he can feel a cold circle of weight pressed there, and then when he's ready, when the time is right, he squeezes the trigger. Pow! The end.

Then he does it again. And when he's finally done, he feels better. He bounds from the bed, shoots his reflection in the wardrobe mirror, shoots a picture of the school swimming team, hits Jimi Hendrix right between the eyes, aims out of the window and hits a workman in the bum. Then he blows the smoke from his pistol, throws it onto the bed disdainfully and walks out of his bedroom, and the memory goes out of focus again.

The gun became a habit, and being purely imagined, it was certainly less damaging than alcohol or cigarettes or Valium or heroin. But it wasn't something you'd want to share with any one. No one would understand. And he himself forgot about it between times. The only time he remembered it was when he was so low, so uncomfortably and vividly self-aware that he wanted to switch himself off as easily as switching off a harsh light or a noisy radio.

As he grew older he came to view it as a sort of meditative practice, the violent and negative equivalent of a mantra. It gave him the power, imaginatively at least, to say no to life. And in saying no, he was also able to go forward and say yes.

His mother was miserable in Swansea and so for three months they tried Mid-Wales again, and they had no car, and his mother's many friends had either left the area or they'd swept the wild days out of their lives and let routine entwine them like cobwebs. Ant had become a social worker and when they'd turned up at his door and seen his newly shorn hair they should have known that everything had changed.

Ant had eyed them like clients instead of friends. He'd lent Ethan's mother fifty quid and she'd taken it, but without thanking him, and when he shut the door on them, she called him a 'bastard' and 'a bald-headed shit'. The money was enough to get them back to Swansea with their clothes and a few other possessions in plastic sacks.

Somehow or other he fell through the years. Fell like Icarus racing past clouds, but adapting himself as he went, modifying parts of his brain and body, inventing a different version of himself as needed. But all the time, now and then, here and there, when it got too bad, he'd put that magic gun in his hand, lift it to his temple. And blow it all away.

When he was nineteen he got a job at the DVLC and a room in a house in Norfolk Terrace. His mother left the area, going first to London where she was miserable, then to Brighton and from there to Scotland where she was briefly married to a man called Gordon Lamb, who despite the name was vicious and violent and spiteful.

She had left one evening with just one suitcase of essentials while her errant husband was at the pub. She had been meaning to go back later for the other things after the dust had settled. But the dust didn't settle for Gordon Lamb and he refused to let her retrieve her belongings. She lost everything; her old clothes – the dresses from Tibet, the Moroccan slippers, the silver trinkets from India, and her record collection, her diaries and letters, drawings Ethan had done when he was little, and a clay chicken he'd made at school, which had brown stripes like a tiger.

Also lost were some black and white pictures that a newspaper photographer had taken long ago and never published. There were pictures of the tepees rising out of a morning mist, and another of everyone gathered in a circle around the bonfire. Ethan's mother tried to pretend that the lost possessions didn't matter, that she'd start over, but for her starting over suddenly meant going back to the place she said she'd been happiest (she must have forgotten that bad winter) and so she returned to Mid Wales.

By then Ethan was twenty-two and lived an unremarkable life for which he was surprisingly grateful. He had owned a succession of old cars. He had some savings in the bank – enough to occasionally bale out his mother, and he'd got some qualifications at night school and planned to go to university. He was seeing a girl called Sarah who was from Kent and in her final year of teacher training. Sarah had seemed to Ethan like the most beautiful creature he had ever seen; with her dark brown hair and green almond-shaped eyes and small fine bones she looked like a Slavic princess. His life might have lacked adventure, but its uneventful path suited him. For the time being.

Sarah was doing supply teaching by the time he was in the final year of his degree in philosophy and politics. They had talked about mortgages and babies and marriage. They stayed in most evenings; Sarah in the middle of the couch with a pile of unmarked papers to her right and marked ones to her left. Ethan at the dining table amidst piles of books and lecture notes, from where he'd occasionally look over at Sarah just to check that she was still there, that he wasn't dreaming. His planned dissertation title was 'The Revolution at Home: Experiments, theories and communes in the nineteen-sixties and seventies.' He had rejected the idea of personal disclosure in the paper, reasoning that it would thwart his objectivity.

His mother wrote to him regularly and he wrote back irregularly, enclosing what money he could spare, as her luck had still not turned. He rarely visited her, finding a million reasons why he couldn't manage it – an overdue essay, a job interview for Sarah, a friend's wedding, a flat tyre on the car. He never lied, but he knew the excuses were often shabby, and so he stuffed crisp new fivers inside his letters as if that would somehow offset his failings.

He got a first for his degree, and the offer of a scholarship to do a PhD in order to develop his research into the sub-cultures of the sixties. Sarah got a permanent teaching job in the history department of a large comprehensive. They put a down payment on a dilapidated house in Brynmill Terrace and spend the weekends tearing down cracked plaster and stripping doors.

In 1998 he spent a total of three and a half hours in his mother's company, meeting her one afternoon in the Penguin Café in Aberystwyth when he was on his way to read a paper at Harlech College. He could have stayed for a night or two, but could not face it.

As they walked along the promenade he had wished that she would dress more smartly, or at least cut her hair. Or wear some make up as her face, no matter how honest, looked ravaged. She seemed so pleased to see him, proud of everything about him, saying several times how tall he seemed, and how very handsome. And because she seemed so happy he made an excuse to escape even earlier than he'd planned. That way, he reasoned, he was softening the blow.

She wrote less often after that. It was as if her life had folded in on itself like a flower closing and there was little to tell in its dark enclosure. Sarah was pregnant and he put off telling his mother the news because he didn't want her to make a fuss..

When the baby was born his mother had sent a parcel of baby clothes, all evidently second-hand, and a pretty, but rather battered, silver rattle that she must have got from a jumble sale. Sarah had wrapped the parcel up again and put it in the cupboard under the stairs where it was very quickly forgotten.

Money was tight, so he got an extension on his doctorate and worked Saturdays and Sundays as a cashier at an all-night petrol station in order to make ends meet. He took his books with him so that he could study in between customers, but he found it hard to concentrate.

One night, at around four o'clock, he lay down out of sight between the aisles of microwave popcorn and tinned soup, and imagined the old black revolver in his hand, but somehow he couldn't find the will to go through with even an imaginary death. Something was stopping him. Louise perhaps? Or the realisation that the imaginary gun and his wishes for oblivion had been up until now, based on a fallacy. His chosen method of suicide was a gun and yet that was an almost impossible choice. Where would he ever get hold of a real gun? What if he'd been dreaming all these years of a razor blade instead? Or pills? He had never really wanted it then. Not once. He'd always wanted to live, despite everything; even now.

He stood up, brushed himself down, went back to his stool by the cash register and found that his mind was wonderfully clear, that the arguments in his essay suddenly fell into place, and noticed that the soft light that was slowly creeping into the morning sky was beautiful.

They made the journey up to his mother's place about once a year in 1999, 2000 and 2001, mostly at Sarah's insistence. But he trimmed each visit down to little more than a day, because he thought that Sarah didn't really want to be there, wouldn't want Louise to be contaminated by the dogs and dirt his mother lived amongst. Sarah agreed to keep the visits short because she thought Ethan was unsettled by his mother's company. Louise played blissfully with the dog, rolled on the floor with him, let him lick her face, and threw spit-slimy rubber balls across the kitchen for him to fetch, then fell asleep in his mother's arms, her small hands clutching her grandma's long rope of greying hair.

His mother had given them a patchwork quilt she'd made. She'd bought herself an old-fashioned treadle machine and it sat in the corner of her living room like a mechanical bird with rivers of half-sewn blood-coloured fabric spewing from its beak. The quilt went in the cupboard with the baby clothes and broken rattle, and was very quickly forgotten.

2

Sarah was pregnant again in 2002 and the baby was due in September – the same month that his mother would turn fifty. His mother wrote begging them to come for her birthday. She was having a little party, she said. She was happy, she said. She'd found someone new; a *good* man.

Ethan had submitted his completed PhD, but his supervisor had suggested that what it lacked was a specific case study. It was a disappointment. He felt like he'd spent years climbing to the top of a glass mountain and now with a tiny puff of breath from his supervisor's lips he'd slid all the way to the bottom again.

But it was not insurmountable. He planned to kill two birds with one stone; go to his mother's, celebrate her birthday, and interview her about the commune, maybe trace Ant and some of the others? Perhaps even find some of the other kids – all of them now grown and gone to who knows where – Pearl and Lotus and Sam and Zeezo.

Zeezo must have changed his name. Surely to God there wasn't a thirty-something still suffering under that curse, but you never knew. Maybe there was still some half-extinct enclave up there holding on to the straws of their lost dreams. Maybe 'the good man' his mother had found was part of the old community. That would make sense.

He left on the sixth, had to stand sideways to put his arms around Sarah and kiss her, then bent and kissed her swollen belly. The second baby wasn't due until the twentieth, and he was only three hours and a mobile phone call away. Sarah handed him a box of presents she'd wrapped for his mother; a pale green pashmina shawl, a fabric covered notebook, the newest Margaret Atwood novel, a basket of lotions and soaps from The Body Shop, twenty skeins of brightly-coloured embroidery silks. And finally, a cassette tape she'd put together of women musicians she thought his mother would like – Gillian Welch, Eva Cassidy, and Joan Osborne.

So that was who Sarah thought his mother was, Ethan considered. Or who she would like her to become.

For his part he had done something that his mother might have thought almost miraculous, except that it had been very simple really. He'd rung the newspaper that had sent the photographer to the commune all those years ago, and spoken to the picture editor. He had a rough idea of the date, and the woman had been the only female staff photographer back then, and he was able to describe the image of the people sitting in a circle around a fire. A small detail, himself as a small boy, running joyously in the background, identified the picture for certain.

He wasn't sure if it was such a good idea really – to give his mother back this vision of the past that had been doubly blighted; once by the disintegration of the commune and its ideals, then again by Gordon Lamb and all he represented. But having got the photos so easily he felt that fate was working some kind of magic.

Considering what was ahead of him, he felt hopeful, happy even. He drove up Carmarthen Road and even the sight of the tower block that had once been his home didn't blight his spirits. The place looked even more run down now. A lot of the corner shops along the way were boarded up and many of the small terraced houses in the area had a beaten, uncared for aspect. He might be heading for his past, but if this was the future; the neglect, the dereliction, then he wanted none of it.

The landscape improved dramatically after Carmarthen, and the coast road north looked unchanged; hills, sheep, and the sea below, grey-blue fading into a smudged edge of sky.

With six month's more work on his thesis, he'd be in a better position to start applying for jobs. The new baby would be settled by then, and so he could apply for posts in Aberystwyth, maybe Lampeter too. They could get a nice place with a bit of land, let the kids run free, breathe fresh air. Get a dog, a cat. Grow organic vegetables. And he could keep an eye on his mother; be a better son.

The only fly in the ointment at that moment was that his fuel light had begun to blink. Over the next hill he found himself driving deeper into a valley where broad-leafed trees formed a shady canopy over the road.

He pulled into the first garage he saw, and parked by the unleaded pump. He got out of the car and put a tenner's worth of petrol in the tank. He went over to the shop, not bothering to lock his doors or wind up the windows, but patted himself down all the same to be certain that he had his wallet and keys on him.

A little tinkling bell announced his arrival as he pushed open the door. He strolled about filling his arms with things he planned to buy; a bottle of fizzy water, a bag of crisps, a bar of chocolate and a kitsch postcard that showed a woman in Welsh costume sitting atop a mountain. He expected the assistant to appear at any minute, but there was no sign of anyone as yet. It amused him to consider how easy it would be to just walk back out of the shop, get in his car and drive off.

He strolled to the counter, put the items he wanted to buy in a little pile near the till, then glanced out at the forecourt where his car was, with its windows open and sunlight bouncing off its windscreen and silver trim. He wondered if there was a brass bell to ring on the counter – the sort you brought your palm down smartly on and had a satisfying dring! sound to it, but there wasn't, so he called out 'Hello' instead. Then he drummed his fingers on the counter trying to do a recognisable rendition of 'Radar Love', which he'd been listening to just before he got out of the car and was buzzing in his head still. He checked his watch, then knocked sharply on the counter, but still no one came.

Which was all very well, as he wasn't in a rush. He was only twenty or thirty minutes from his mother's house now, and it was a beautiful day, but what if he was supposed to be somewhere urgently? What then?

But not every garage was like this; it would be ignorant of him to believe that. He refused to believe it. If they came to live here they would not be doing it as city slickers always dwelling on the countryside's weak points. But he would, he thought, probably avoid this garage in the future, at least if he was in a hurry. On the other hand, he reasoned, this place was probably understaffed and run down precisely because no one came here. There must be a bigger petrol station nearby, which gave discounts and free gifts and Nectar points and all that hullabaloo.

He called out again, louder this time, 'anybody there? Hello-o?' and sighing, he reached into his pocket for his wallet, opened it and pulled out a ten and a five. It was more than the goods and petrol came to, but the loss of a couple of pounds here or there wasn't going to kill him, and he needed to get on the road again. He placed the two notes side by side in the middle of the counter where they could be seen immediately. Then he went for the door, which tinkled gently as he opened it.

A soft breeze blew in his face, carrying the scent of cut grass mixed with petrol. He turned to see if an assistant was finally coming, and was just in time to see his two bank notes waft gracefully across the countertop in the draft of the open door, and disappear behind it.

'Shit,' he murmured under his breath. He considered leaving anyway. They'd find the money surely? But then maybe not, and besides they might not connect the loose money on the floor with the customer who helped himself to ten pound's worth of petrol and legged it. They needed to know that someone honest had been there, that not everyone was going to take advantage. He walked back, called out again, this time very loudly, and then feeling like a thief, he leaned over the counter to retrieve the cash. The five was lying in the middle of the floor, but the ten was nowhere to be seen.

He leaned over more, praying that the assistant wouldn't choose that precise moment to come into the shop. He ran his eye carefully over the floor; there was a familiar mess behind there, dust bunnies and cardboard boxes and cellophane wraps – no point cleaning what couldn't be seen.

The ten pound note must have gone further or got lodged somewhere. He leaned even further over, so that his feet no longer touched the floor and his belly lay flat on the counter top.

It was at that moment that two things happened at once. He noticed that what he had taken to be a discarded shoe laying on its side behind some large cardboard cartons had a foot and a grey-socked ankle inside it. He thought briefly that this might be some practical joke; but as his heart began to pound in earnest, he heard a sudden noise behind him. It was an urgent, rushing, sound and it seemed to bear down on him out of nowhere. He struggled clumsily to pull himself upright, but as soon as his feet had found the floor again, his cheek was slammed down hard on the cold Formica surface of the counter. Something was pressing hard on his back – a knee or elbow, and someone or something he couldn't see was holding his head firmly in place.

He could hear breathing; heavy and belaboured, but there was something odd about the sound, as if someone were breathing into a paper bag. He strained his eye upward, irresistibly, to see what this thing was that held him, and saw only an out of focus blur of something gaudy and shiny and inhuman.

He pressed one foot hard against the floor to give himself leverage and tried to jerk himself upright, but the man slammed him down again harder than before. Ethan felt that there was even a certain grim pleasure in the muffled grunt the man made as he did it, and that frightened him more than anything else. To be attacked by a thief, no matter how ruthless, was one thing, but a sadist; that was another thing entirely.

He lay still, and tried to convey submission, force a message of defeat from his tense muscles into the man's stronger ones. He tried to breathe more slowly, thought about the ante-natal classes he and Sarah had been going to these last few months; the deep breathing, the panting, the soothing nursery rhymes you should chant inside your head to escape the pain.

The man had shifted position slightly, as if lifting himself off in order to reach something. Ethan moved his head an inch or so and managed to catch a glimpse of his attacker, except that instead of a face he saw a plastic mask; a Mickey Mouse one with a happy grin and big round black ears. The cartoon grin seemed suddenly maniacal and monstrous, the opposite of cute or whatever it should have been.

Maybe Ethan should say something, reason with the guy, but what do you say? What would his opening gambit be?

The first word would be 'listen'. He could feel it waiting there on the tip of his tongue.

'Listen. I won't tell.' Or 'Listen, my wife is going to have a baby'. Or maybe his first word would be 'please'.

The man shifted again, and the muffled, echoing noise of his breathing came closer until it was hot and moist by Ethan's ear.

'You dumb fuck,' he hissed, 'you fuck brain.'

'Please,' Ethan said, and he had never felt so pathetic before in his entire life.

There was a moment of stillness then, and Ethan sensed that the man was gazing off somewhere, considering what to do next, enjoying the power he held, the beautiful sense of his all-powerful strength and might.

Ethan thought that if he could make himself as still as possible, if he could manage to not antagonise the man, then maybe everything would be all right. He wished at that moment to erase himself from the picture, to leave behind only a shell or mannequin that presented no threat.

Then time seemed to collapse in on itself and the light in the room suddenly changed – maybe the sun had gone behind a cloud or the man had moved so that he blocked it.

Ethan heard a sound, a sharp click like a briefcase lock opening or closing and then he felt something touch his right temple, something cold and hard, and, yes, round and hollow like the muzzle of a gun. The sound he'd heard must have been the weapon being cocked.

Here was the thing he'd dreamed about a hundred times. Something he'd once abstractly believed he'd wanted, and now it seemed like those terrible thoughts in the past hadn't been desires, but shadows of the future on his fragile skin, reminders of mortality. Premonitions.

'I should kill you now,' the man said in a voice that was calm and reasonable, 'I should just blow your head off.'

He pressed harder, pushed his knee deeper into Ethan's back, hurting him, squeezing his chest so that it was hard to breathe.

'But maybe, you're not worth the trouble.'

And saying that he lifted himself off, and the place on Ethan's head where the cold metal had been, though still numb, grew warmer.

Ethan did not move. He sensed the figure just beyond him, imagined the gun still trained at his head. It was a strain to stay in that awkward position without the weight of someone holding him there. He let one foot slyly adjust itself so that he was almost half-standing again. He could just about see part of the window and the forecourt beyond. He could see a portion of his car's fender and the wheel rim, and as he watched the sun came out, throwing dazzling light here and black leafy shadows there.

The silence endured, and Ethan's body ached.

He lifted his head, craning his neck and pushing up almost imperceptibly with his shoulders, barely daring to look again at that insane Mickey Mouse mask; not wanting to see the gun which up until now he had only felt. And all the time he was bracing himself to receive a bullet in much the same way that you'd tighten your muscles against a punch. Except that with a gun the action was completely useless; his muscles might as well have been butter.

But there was no one there. He lifted his head completely, then raised his body, twisted around, scanned the shop, and still he saw no one.

He touched his temple where the muzzle had been pressed and he detected a faint indentation of skin that bulged, soft and warm, in its centre. He pushed at the bulge gently, testing it, thinking about the soft spot on a baby's skull, the fontanel, a little vulnerable place in the bone, which with time, would heal over.

He allowed himself a minute to stand there, pulling air deep into his lungs, listening to the little signals and reports which his body was sending him about the battering he'd had, and revelling in every tweak and ache and pain as each seemed to confirm that he was very much alive. No, not just alive, but more alive than he had ever been; would ever be.

True Crime

As in all good stories, theirs began innocently enough with a hardworking and studious mother and a dreamy doe-eyed daughter. The mother was lecturing part time and doing a PhD about horror movies. Even when talking about a film that was watched purely for pleasure, she would still pepper her language with words like 'genre', 'auteur' and 'mise-en-scene' – which was her way of proving that she was not seduced by story alone. Though she is.

Equally, she might, when discussing films like *Carrie* or *The Shining*, use terms and ideas from feminism or psychology. Deconstructing *Carrie* lets her sleep at night – mostly. But fear can be a small strange chink of light beyond a curtain. Or an unfamiliar sound at four in the morning. Or the anguished shout overheard in the middle of the afternoon; the cry of pain which cannot be seen amongst the lawns and hedges and regimented tulips of her neighbour's gardens – though by the time she reaches the window there is nothing to be seen at all. Her breath fogs the glass. Her heart slows. The day expands. The soundtrack is *so* deliberately normal – a washing machine, a Radio One DJ talking nonsense, pneumatic drills, a cat bounding crazily from one end of the house to the other, its claws skittering to a sudden halt on the tiles in the kitchen – that something *must* come of it.

These things she doesn't talk about. Not to her daughter. Not to anyone. It wasn't always like this, and yet it feels as if it was. As if the threat the mother senses, has been out there somewhere in the world, waiting for its chance.

If luck is a lady, then fate is the hooded assailant lurking in the bushes with a pair of hi-tech night vision goggles. Fate is something invented by Thomas Harris; a Hannibal Lector, a murderer without a soul, someone who is the product of the late twentieth century. Jack the Ripper doesn't really compare, he's almost quaint by comparison.

Some nights she has trouble sleeping, other nights she is torn out of sleep by terrible nightmares that leave her trembling and exhausted. When this happens she gets out of bed, goes down to her study and writes notes that describe the physical sensations her body undergoes when she is afraid. Sometimes she finds herself thinking that her fixation with horror movies might actually wind up summoning bad things out of the darkness because she's tempted fate once too often. But then she pulls herself together and muses on how that is just the way those films are meant to make you think, and she laughs at herself.

And then, and here's the twist, she realises that this is *exactly* how the modern horror plot would go. Other times she just thinks she's going very quietly, very subtly mad.

And how would one know if one was going mad? That is the awful thing. She is certain that if she was, her daughter would tell her. But there again could her words penetrate the madness? Wouldn't she be like the loopy old dame in *Sunset Boulevard* misreading the reporter's camera flashes as studio lights? But, she supposed, if she was that far gone, that deluded, would it matter?

She caught herself thinking this and glanced around the room as if to reassure herself. There was the usual pile of books next to the computer, *The Cinema Book*, *Women and Cinema, Film and Psychology*, and *The Horror Reader*. She reached out to touch them, to reassure herself of the solid reality of the objects around her, but thought better of it, touched the desk's wooden surface instead.

She was tired, but in a wired up, jittery way, as if the night had electrified her with its store of endless silence, endless dark. One more cigarette then bed. Maybe a small glass of whisky and then she'd be done.

She switched off the computer; put her empty glass and the full ashtray in the kitchen, while the cat curled itself around her ankles, desperate for attention although its food bowl was full. She ran her hand against its head and the cat flopped on to its back, showing its soft belly, enticing her. Without thinking she ran a hand over its chest, enjoying the sensation of its silky fur and the idea of their mutual love. But the cat had other ideas and caught her off guard, suddenly grasping the unprotected hand between its paws and sinking its teeth in, making her cry out in pain.

Then just as quickly it let go and bounded down the hall and halfway up the stairs, from where it watched her by popping its head through the banisters, wild-eyed and stupidly crazy.

You could see why cats in particular were associated with witches; all that carefully washed fur; the pretty face, the delicate way of sitting; front paws just so, but concealing needles and razors and viciousness. Even the witch would get it sometimes.

She studied her hand; some superficial scratches on the back and wrist, but worse, there was one deep puncture wound in the tender spot between her ring and little finger. Blood pulsed up forming a small dome, precious and ruby red.

She didn't lick or suck her wound the way some people did; she hated the taste of blood, the iron tang of it. So she dabbed a spot of Germolene on it then covered it with a plaster. And realized as she did it that she had shaken off, momentarily at least, that fear of something coming at her in the night. She knew that tonight she'd sleep. Something had already got her. Something had drawn blood and so was sated until the next night.

The next day was a Saturday and she woke grudgingly, with a headache and blocked sinuses, angry and regretful of the previous night's excess. Fear does not get drowned with whisky, only muted, but the morning's light was welcome nonetheless.

She went downstairs to the kitchen, filled the kettle

and put two mugs ready. The cat was speaking to her, giving its questioning two note call, 'Meow-ow?' then purring frantically when she picked it up and draped it over her left shoulder. But as soon as she had opened its sachet of food, it scrambled to be released.

The kettle throbbed briefly, then switched itself off and she poured the boiling water into the mugs and waited for the tea to steep. The cat was now arranging itself above the litter tray; its body seemed taut, acrobatic, as it strained to hold its pose. It stared at her with a narrow distant gaze, and a long shining turd dropped, and then settled in the hard white crumbs of the box.

It seemed to have a preference for taking its morning shit while she was there to see it. To smell it. But at least it used its tray; the last cat had favoured the plant pots, but that cat was long gone.

She carried the mugs upstairs and put one on her bedside table, then went quietly into her daughter's room. She stood there for a moment looking at her child's sweet face upon the pillow, lost in sleep. Her hair fell across one cheek and over one closed eye. Her lashes were long and black and thick, which combined with her big brown eyes, got her into all sorts of trouble. Boys – well not only boys unfortunately – thought she was giving them the come on, when her luminous stare was actually only this, an accidental accumulation of physical attributes.

The girl was fifteen, sixteen in the autumn. The child she had been had gone, except for now, in moments like these.

The mother put the cup on the small table near the girl's bed, and sat on the edge of the low mattress.

'Sweetie,' she said and reached forward to touch the girl's shoulder. But her daughter's eyes flashed open and the shoulder rolled away out of reach.

'I heard you come into the room, what were you doing?'

This was as bad as when the cat bit her.

The girl groaned an objection at the intrusion.

'The class is at eleven, darling, so I thought...'

'Yeah, yeah....'

The mother went out of the room, spurned and furious. She shut the door loudly, not quite slamming it, but near enough.

She went and got back into her own bed; it was warm under the covers and her mug of tea was there on the bedside table, but these seemed hollow comforts now.

She was due to give a lecture to her tutorial group on Monday, which she planned to call, 'The last, last girl, the end of horror, from *Halloween* to *Scream*.'

It was meant to be about the debunking of horror, a demonstration of how once a formula can be perceived, an audience can no longer engage with their fear. That was the theory anyway.

The mother picked up a small spiral bound notebook and began to write.

* * *

The girl feels as if she has lived in this long mirrored room for half her life, which in some ways is true. She started at The Sylvia Bennett Dance Academy when she was six, and she's attended every Saturday morning ever since. But there comes a point when you lose your obedience – why should she do this if she doesn't want to? You carry on for the sake of hope, for the idea that one day you will be a dancer, but then the hope starts to fade too. These days she comes for the exercise and to see her friends in the class, and finally for a quiet life.

All of which makes for guilt.

She doesn't mean to snap at her mother, though she finds her mother's anger easier to bear than her pain. Lately she has managed to make her mother weep no less than six times. She knows this because she has acquired a new habit; that of reading her mother's diary.

She also keeps a diary and is certain that her mother has never read it. Her mother is keen on issues of trust and honesty and privacy.

Sometimes her mother uses her absent father as an example of someone who would breach the boundaries of privacy.

'Your father read my letters,' the mother would sometimes say to illustrate her point, 'letters that I'd received and also letters that I'd asked him to post for me. I mean, there I was in hospital, confined to a bed afraid that I'd lose you and he did that!'

The daughter didn't like hearing this. Or rather she didn't like hearing it over and over.

'I don't think you fully understand,' her mother would say, 'it's the *betrayal*. You can't understand. You wouldn't understand unless it happened to you. Which I hope it never does.'

Nag. Nag. Nag.

She walks to her class at the YMCA while her mother parks the car. They'll meet up later for lunch in Café Mambo on the Kingsway; her mother will have been sitting there for an hour or more by the time she gets there. Her mother will be chain-smoking, creating her own protective fog of privacy; she'll have her glasses on and they'll keep slipping to the end of her nose and she'll be scribbling frantically in some notebook or other. Her mother would have appreciated some extra arms like the god Vishnu, but then she'd probably try to do even more all at the same time.

Michelle thinks this as she climbs the stairs to the dance studio. There are four flights; plenty of thinking time. She walks slowly, though the stairs aren't a challenge at all. She's young and fit, as weightless as a leaf, but her mind has been resisting lately and frankly, she can't really be arsed.

The greetings among her friends when she gets to the changing room are equally muted, there is a rolling of eyes when the dancing teacher tries to chivvy them along as they trudge drearily into the studio.

But something is there still in each of the girls, simmering under the surface and only coming to life when they are positioned at the barre; when the mirrors are there to count and recount each movement of the exercise. By the time they are dancing, it is fully alive, like bright sunlight bouncing off a shiny object.

There are glass doors at the end of the room that lead to the back stairs. It's where the mothers used to stand when they were little, and had to be collected from the class. Except that most of the mothers would show up early in order to spy on the last moments. To catch a glimpse of their own precious darlings as they attempted to embody the grace of a swan, or the beauty of a flower.

The mothers had looks on their faces as though they were both starved and stuffed to the gills at the same time. Her mother was usually late, disheveled and distracted; no less loving than the other mothers, just different.

A few weeks ago, just after Christmas, Michelle noticed a figure standing behind the door. She was dancing at the time, moving fast across the sprung floor with nine other girls. All of them with peasant skirts Velcro-ed over their leotards. She saw whoever it was in a flash; as a still point. She noticed because it was too early for a parent to show up and because the shape was unmistakably male. A man's silhouette; tall, slim, and broad shouldered. He lingered for six, seven minutes, and then he was gone.

The second week she noticed him again and pretended for a while, as she danced, that he was a talent scout for a film company and he was searching for that one special girl to play the role of the dancer. Or something. In her fantasy she'd always have to leave the class right at that moment. 'You don't know how long it's taken me to find you,' he'd say and he'd have a car waiting, a very new, very expensive car; the sort that people would stop to look at. The only problem with this fantasy was that to make it real she had to somehow accommodate her mother, and that brought everything crashing back to earth.

The next time she saw him, she pretended that she had a problem with her ballet shoes. She knew she would get snapped at by the dance teacher for failing to thoroughly check them in the first place, but that didn't matter.

She sat on one of the benches near the door, but not quite near enough to be obvious. She undid the ribbon and unwound it from her ankle, then rubbed her foot and dared to take a look at the man. He was watching her even though Eleanor Phillips was doing her Giselle at that moment, plucking at the floorboards on her points, tilting her exquisite face to the light.

When their eyes met, he smiled. She smiled back, but turned away quickly to hide her blush.

She refastened her shoe, preparing herself not to dance, but to look at him again, to smile properly this time. She felt him watching her as she fussed with the ribbon, making sure it was straight, but when she looked up, there was no one there and the glass door seemed far away. Further away than it had been before, and also more scuffed and smeared than she had ever noticed.

Last week, he had smiled and she had smiled back, and he had mouthed a word at her and she'd mouthed it back, 'Hi.'

Then he lifted his palm and winked.

Not a dirty wink like old men and men on building sites did, but a friendly, gleaming wink that made her tummy flutter and her heart beat faster.

He was older than her. She had guessed he was perhaps twenty-six or seventy-seven. She knew he wasn't a talent scout, but that didn't seem to matter anymore. What mattered was that he had seemed so nice, that he was sort of good looking, that he was mature, but mostly it was that he liked her. She was the one from all the girls there that he had chosen.

She had waved back and he had begun to mouth other words, but then she saw him turn abruptly and disappear. The outline of a woman replaced his shape behind the glass, and ten minutes later the class finished.

She dressed hurriedly, throwing on her clothes carelessly, not bothering to do anything with her hair. She thought that she might find him waiting for her.

She had felt concern for him. What had he wanted to say? Why had he had to go so abruptly? What if he was falling in love with her but thought she didn't like him? What if this was their one chance?

* * *

Her mother was lighting another cigarette and checking her watch. She scribbled a few more notes and a reminder to herself, 'Research long-term physiological effects of fear. Symbolism of birds. Buy coffee, lemons, wine, chicken.'

* * *

This week the dance mistress seemed to be continually asking her to do things that made watching the door impossible. She'd been moved to the end of the studio for some obscure reason and she'd had to be the boy to Eleanor's girl; holding Eleanor's waist lightly as she turned, then counting their way through the jumps because she sure as hell couldn't lift the other girl. And once she was caught craning her head around to see the door and got yelled at and so didn't dare try again.

She didn't see him. Not once. But had no way of knowing if this was because he hadn't been there, or if she had just missed him.

In the changing room she undressed angrily and hardly spoke a word to anyone. Her two friends, after getting a dose of the glum treatment, more or less ignored her, which had the effect of making her feel even worse.

She put on the clothes she had so carefully chosen that morning; her favourite jeans, the black boots, the tangerine coloured T-shirt with the three buttons which she could leave open so as to look sexy. She put on more make up; a second coating of mascara so that her lashes looked even more long and thick than they already were, then lip gloss, though she hated how it made her mouth feel sticky as if she'd been eating sugary doughnuts.

* * *

The mother had been sitting at the back of the café in the gloom, but now when she glanced up to look out for her daughter; she noticed that the sun was shining and that there were tables outside. On impulse she gathered up her books, cigarettes and jacket and hurried to the front. She stopped by the counter to order another coffee and let the staff know she had changed tables. The waiter gave her that dull open-mouthed look that told her she was an old insignificant pain in the ass sort of customer who had taken up too much time, space and energy already. She knew he'd buck up when her daughter appeared, they usually did.

As always she considered the psychological truth of this; her own invisibility, her light rapidly diminishing as her daughter's flame gathered strength. She opened her notebook, uncapped her pen and wrote:

Bad mothers as a site for abjection in horror.
1. Carrie/Psycho (mother too strong)
2. The Shining (mother too weak)
Male castration fears v. desire/Hitchcock's bad women/
fairy tales etc

Then she stared into space, feeling tragic, and yet aware that she was too fat to be really tragic.

* * *

Michelle's two friends were in a hurry, so she told them to go without her; she'd see them later maybe, or in the week, or next Saturday. She finished dressing slowly as if the light in the changing room was thickening and becoming glutinous, and she had to strain her muscles to make them obey her.

She was the last student to leave.

'Is everything alright?' the dance mistress asked when she saw her.

'Yeah.'

'Where are Sarah and Karen?'

'They've gone.'

The teacher waved her off, concealing her concern. The girl looked ill and had dark shadows under her eyes. Her friends had gone without her and she'd lost her joie de vivre. And you never saw that mother of hers, though the teacher could still vividly picture her lumbering up the stairs; a fine sheen of sweat on her face, out of breath, overweight, smelling of cigarettes and Patchouli in equal measure.

The dance mistress had never really forgiven Michelle's mother for an occasion long ago when she had read a book throughout an entire dance recital, only stopping to watch the show when her own daughter was on stage. Michelle had tried to explain and apologize for her mother even though she was only seven or eight at the time, 'Mummy's doing a PhD as well as being a mummy,' she'd said, but the words seemed clumsy in the child's mouth, like something regurgitated.

All of the girls were vulnerable. It was their age. You had to watch what you said to them these days, make sure none of them were starving themselves or throwing up or whatever.

She went to the windows and looked down just in time to see Michelle pass by on the pavement directly below. As she watched, she saw that instead of the girl's mother, a man had fallen into step beside her. She couldn't see his face, but on the crown of his head you could clearly see the beginnings of a bald patch. As they crossed the road towards the arcade, he put a protective arm around her shoulder.

'So her father is back on the scene,' the dance teacher thought, 'that's got to change things,' and then she thought fondly of her own father; of his bow ties and cigars and the cream-coloured pigskin gloves he wore for driving, and she couldn't imagine how life would have been without him.

* * *

'So, coffee or tea?'

The man had seemed to spring out of nowhere and now he was by her side, walking close enough so that their elbows touched, and he was smiling.

'I'm sorry, I don't —,' she said to cover her confusion.

She wondered what she was meant to say. Had he said hello before this? She couldn't remember, but it didn't matter did it?

'Which do you prefer, Michelle?'

That seemed an easier question to answer, she didn't have to think about its meaning, or what the implication was, or what was happening. She could answer that, but she couldn't remember them exchanging names. Had she told him her name was Michelle? Had she forgotten his name so quickly? But wasn't this confusion a sign of true love; quite normal really.

He had an accent of some sort, it was very slight, something partially diluted by years in Wales perhaps – maybe Irish, or perhaps Scottish?

'I, well, tea I suppose...'

'Okay, tea it is. Let's cross here.'

She was going to cross the road anyway, but now he was beside her, and he'd put his hand first on the small of her back, and then around her shoulder. That's what men did, she thought, they guided girls across the road and opened doors for them. They looked after women. And they also swept them off their feet, which seemed to be what was happening now. Not literally of course, but it was sudden, the way it is in books and movies. Love at first sight.

Of course, he had kept his arm around her once they were safely across, and as they walked along the Kingsway his arm had slipped so it was around her waist, which tickled a bit. She wondered if anyone would see them. She wanted someone to see them. Had he said hello first? She just couldn't remember. She smiled the same fixed smile she wore when she was dancing and her feet hurt.

At the corner of Union Street he began to turn right, and meekly, feeling the press of his hand on her body, she also turned – as a horse will turn when a knee is pressed into its flank.

'Kardomah then, is it?'

'Oh, well...'

'No? Don't fancy the Kardomah?'

'Um, no, I mean, I'm supposed to meet my mother....'

He stopped walking and took his arm from around her to scratch his head. The place where his arm had been felt colder suddenly. She could see him clearly now. Close up she noticed that he had some acne scars, that he needed to shave, that the whites of his eyes were not very bright, and that he was a bit older than she had thought. His face had lost every trace of boyishness and he was broad-shouldered, lean and angular. The colour of his eyes though, was blue – like a china bird.

'I'm sorry,' she said to him.

'A quick cup of tea,' he said, 'you've got time for a quick cup of tea, haven't you?'

He reached into his pocket, pulled out a half-smoked cigarette, lit it and took quick drags off it. He held it between a thumb and forefinger, frowning and avoiding her eyes.

She looked at her watch, she was already twenty minutes late, but she'd been later than that before now and her mother had barely noticed.

'Oh, all right then,' she said in a sudden rush, and the shadow immediately lifted from his face. He threw the cigarette down, and grabbed her hand and held it all the way to the café.

'My name's Joseph,' he said as they went along, squeezing her hand, 'but you can call me Joe.'

* * *

Question: Is Carrie stigmatized because of her mother, or has her mother become monstrous because of Carrie's telekinetic powers?

Question: What is the significance of blood and ritual in Carrie?

The mother sat considering the two essay questions she'd jotted down. She knew that there was no real answer, or not an answer in a straightforward way. What the students were meant to do was go through the motions, show their thinking and their knowledge. But for what? She'd spent the last 10 weeks lecturing them about precisely this, and now in essay form she was supposed to listen to her own ideas being bounced back at her like so many echoes. Maybe she'd been teaching for too long, and was not so much stressed out, as jaded – though perhaps it amounted to the same thing.

She checked her watch. Twelve thirty-five. Michelle was late. Again.

* * *

'Would you like to see a fil-um, Michelle?' Joe said, and she stared at him, marveling at the strange – and to her ears silly – twist he'd given to the last word.

'Where are you from?' she asked.

He seemed to dislike the question, but answered anyway.

'Cork. Now answer my question, darling.'

She stared down at the surface of the table; it was white with a pattern of black coffee beans. Her mother had told her that they had had these tables forever, since the sixties at least, but somehow Michelle couldn't quite believe it. She'd been brought here by her grandmother for afternoon tea when she was very little, and now here she was almost grown up, on her first proper date. How could so much change, when the tables remained the same?

'Yes, I'd love to go to the cinema with you.'

'Grand,' he'd said, 'that'll be grand.'

Then he promised to ring her later, and let her go to meet her mother. He stayed at the table in the Kardomah lighting a cigarette in lieu of kissing her goodbye.

She had been hurrying, but by the time she drew level with the bus stop opposite the church, she could see her mother sitting outside Café Mambo, and so she relaxed her pace and gave herself time to prepare. A part of her wanted to tell her mother everything, but the other part wanted to keep this day, and this man buried away like a sweet and exotic secret that could neither be explained nor shared in any way. So she said nothing and the day passed in its ordinary way, even though inside she was buzzing with dreams and ideas that were as restless as a swarm of black flies.

That night Michelle and her mother watched *Equus* on DVD, but both were secretly distracted – her mother by an idea that had been forming in her head for some time now; that she should offer her resignation at the college where she had taught for the last four years, and concentrate for perhaps a year or so on completing her PhD. Michelle was watching the phone and waiting for it to ring.

Halfway through the film, the mother put the DVD on pause and said, 'Tea?'

'Yeah, I'll be right there now,' Michelle said on her way up to her room. Once there she stood and looked at herself in the full-length mirror for a long time.

The phone rang, and while Michelle raced to get it, by the time she was halfway down the stairs, she could hear her mother saying, 'Hello? Hello?'

She stopped and listened, expecting at any moment for her mother to call her to the phone, but instead there was a pause, then her mother repeated hello another three times, before she replaced the receiver. Michelle walked into the living room and waited, feigning an air of disinterest.

'Wrong number?' Michelle asked.

'Heavy breather,' her mother said, then, 'ready for the film?'

'Oh, I dunno...'

'Well, we don't have to watch it now.'

'I should read my book for English.'

The mother, because she could not help herself, looked crestfallen.

'Do you mind?' Michelle said, seeing the look.

'No, no. Some other time, eh?'

Michelle went back to her room and switched off the overhead light and stood in the darkness gazing at the empty street and willing him to appear.

Her mother sat and stared at the TV. It had been an odd moment to pause the action for the screen showed a middle-aged man and woman both frozen in the act of sitting down opposite one another. Each of them was bent awkwardly, bodies folded above their respective chairs, but looking more as if they were in the midst of some curious country dance which involved bowing and curtseying.

The silent phone call worried the mother. She was ex-directory, but nothing was foolproof. She remembered that line from a poem by Sylvia Plath; something vivid and memorable about a black telephone and voices which couldn't worm through.

She knew she couldn't leave her job, not unless she found another. Her savings would last six months, nine at the most, and completing the PhD guaranteed nothing, nada, zilch. It was useless. She was trapped.

* * *

Michelle was certain that Joe had phoned that Saturday night, but that something in her mother's tone had rendered him unable to speak, had made him go away. Maybe he wouldn't even try to phone again, but even if he didn't, she was certain he would be there to meet her at the YMCA the following week and she could hardly bear the wait. Time seemed suddenly like a long dull bridge that passed over a chasm of time.

So she trudged wearily through the week: in the evenings she tried to stay close to the phone, did her homework on her lap while her mother watched more horror films with the volume turned down low. These films were rubbish, her mother said, and Michelle could see that that was true, because if you only half-watched, they could not bind you with their spell.

At school she hinted to her friends that she was in love, and sighed dreamily but refused to answer direct questions. 'Wouldn't you like to know?' she said more than once and smiled a secret smile. She told her mother she didn't want to meet her after the dance class; that she'd probably go shopping with friends, or to the cinema maybe. She'd ring if she needed a lift. And after the shops and the cinema she might go back to Sarah's house. Or she and Sarah might both go to Karen's for a sleepover. Or maybe everyone would go to Cassie's.

And after she said it, there it was again, that look of hurt on her mother's face. It was enough to drive you crazy.

* * *

The mother had had phone calls like this before. The mechanical noise of the ringing wrenching you out of your sleep, dragging you from your studies, wringing you out of the bath, and then when you picked up, only silence. Except that it wasn't quite silence, rather it was a distant quiet rushing sound like the small ocean that lapped upon the distant shores of a shell.

But all that had been so long ago, when Michelle was only four or five. Since then she'd had her number changed and gone ex-directory. But she still remembered the fear she'd felt back then, the sense that she'd had to hide herself away. As if she was the one who had done something wrong; as if she were the sinner who must be tormented and punished.

And underlying the fear there was also guilt; for it was her weakness that had let in the monster, and beyond the guilt, underneath her skin was this visceral version of herself, this ugly, fleshy, too abundant self that hungered and stuffed her maw with what she thought then had been love, but was in reality a neediness that could never be satisfied.

The truth was she had hated herself then, but hadn't known it. And now she hated herself for not knowing. Stupid, stupid, stupid.

One more phone call like that and she'd get the number changed again.

* * *

On Friday night her mother attended an evening class in computer studies, but this week she hadn't wanted to go. Michelle nagged and begged her to go, using the logic her mother more usually used against her. It was only two hours; she'd feel bad if she didn't go; giving up was for losers. Her mother could hardly refuse, and Michelle was left to continue her silent vigil by the telephone.

At nine it finally rang, but it was only her mother to say that she would be a little late as it was someone's birthday and they were going to the pub, and it would be rude if she didn't have at least one drink with them.

Michelle felt that Joe would know everything about their schedule; that he would understand that the best time to ring was Friday night because her mother was out. Her mother was normally home by about half past nine, so he only had twenty or so minutes left in which to ring. Michelle needed to pee, but made herself stay by the phone, half-heartedly watching a reality show on cable, and checking her watch every few minutes or so.

At twenty past ten Michelle had got up and was headed for the door on her way to the bathroom when the phone rang again startling her.

'Hello?' she said aware of a tremor in her voice.

There was a pause, though she sensed him there at the other end, 'Joe? Hello, Joseph?'

'So you remembered my name,' he said, and Michelle smiled and let herself sink down the wall, until she was huddled on the floor, nursing the phone against her cheek.

'Mm,' was all she could manage to say.

'Can you get away, darling?' he asked.

'When?'

'Now, of course.'

'Oh. I don't think so...'

'Is your Mammy there?'

She resented the word 'mammy', and the implication.

'My mother isn't here, no.'

'Well, then...'

'But she'll be here soon'

There was a long silence then and Michelle imagined him considering this and smoking thoughtfully with his eyes narrowed.

'I love you,' he said all in a rush and the next thing Michelle knew he had abruptly hung up, and she could hear something at the door; a step, then the noise of a key in the lock, and her mother calling her name.

She replaced the receiver as her mother came into the room.

'Someone on the phone?'

'No. Or yes, but wrong number.'

Her mother frowned, 'Are you sure?'

'Yes, it was someone asking for...' she hesitated, 'for Joe. Or something.'

'Oh, okay then.'

* * *

Later that night in her notebook, the mother wrote, 'What is fear then, but a message passed from hand to hand like

114

an Olympic flame? Or at least this is true in regard to a fear of the unknown, nameless terrors; the crippling adaptation of foresight or apprehension. The closing off and locking away – Rapunzel in her tower is vulnerable precisely because of the knowledge kept from her. Ignorance is not bliss.'

She was tired by then, and had drunk a large glass of burgundy rather too quickly when she and the rest of the class were in the *No Sign Wine Bar*. She had asked for a small one, but it seemed bad manners to attempt to undo the mistake, or do anything but quite literally swallow it. She didn't quite understand what the words she had written referred to; the research she was doing on *Carrie* or her own life. Maybe there was no difference.

She had suspected that her daughter was lying to her earlier about the phone call, but did not feel she could confront her, or even should for that matter; her daughter was as much entitled to her privacy as anyone.

* * *

The door to the living room was wide open, and the only light in there came from the TV screen, but Michelle could see her mother on the couch fast asleep with a pen still in her hand. Her notebook must have slipped from the couch, because it lay on the floor propped up on its edges like the roof of a house. She tiptoed into the room, turned down the sound on the TV and then with infinite care, she draped a tartan blanket over her mother. She knew her mother was sleeping soundly; she had already slept through the noisy end of that film she'd been watching for the umpteenth time, had dozed on despite the screams and the pounding music and amplified heartbeats at its end. Hadn't woken even when the phone rang again at gone twelve. Hadn't stirred as Michelle had whispered her agreement to slip from the house in order to meet Joe.

Michelle pulled the door of the living room quietly closed behind her, and in the hall she put on her trainers and coat. She stopped only to look at herself briefly in the mirror by the front door, applied another layer of the sticky lip-gloss, then pulled up the fur-trimmed hood of her jacket against the night. Joe had said he would be in an aqua green Escort down on the main road a few minutes' walk away, and that he'd keep the motor running, just so she'd be sure it was him.

Her shoes made no sound on the pavements as she walked quickly to the end of the street. It was a moonless night, overcast and misty. Somewhere in the distance she heard the steady rush of traffic, broken only by the sharp cry of a fox. Her breath preceded her in little clouds like cigarette smoke. Later, when he took a cigarette packet from his pocket she'd ask him if she could have one, and she'd hold it between her first and second fingers and tilt her head back to blow smoke at the ceiling the way she'd seen her friend do it; showing off her pretty neck, closing her eyes like someone in a film when they did *it*.

As she drew closer to the main road, she felt that she had never been happier; thought that she could not ever feel more joy and love than she did at this very moment. And luckily did not know that in this last assumption she had never been more right.

Letters to Neil

6th January, 1990

Dear Neil,

Well, I suppose you must be wondering who is writing to you from Aberystwyth. Unless of course, you've already turned the letter over to see what name is at its end, in which case all of this is meaningless. So I'll say quickly now that it's Anne. Remember me? I used to work in the Farmer's Arms when you used to come for the poetry readings.

I was the friend of Jenny's with the red hair – me that is, not Jenny. She was Neville's girlfriend and they lived in Talybont.

Anyway, I bumped into a mutual friend recently and he gave me your address. I might be moving up to London myself soon, so I thought I'd drop you a line. Alex also said to say 'Hi' and he's back at the farmhouse if you want to get in touch.

Hope to hear from you soon,
Anne

15th January, 1990

Hello again Neil,

Thought I'd just drop you this postcard as I forgot to mention that Alex said to tell you he's having a party on Feb 10th and that there's plenty of room if you want to stay the night, so long as you bring a sleeping bag.

Bye,
Anne

P.S. Hope you like this card – I always remember the night when you were talking about Dylan Thomas. Do you still like his poetry?

1st February, 1990

Hi Neil,

Alex said he got your letter and that you said to say hello to me. He also said you sounded pretty busy, what with your poetry and the job at the arts centre, not to mention the film script. Wow, life sounds really exciting in London, I can't wait to get up there myself.

Aberystwyth is okay, though there's not much going on here really. I'm still working as a barmaid so that gives me lots of material for my stories, though they're not very good – not a patch on yours I'm sure.

I'd love to read some of your stuff, maybe when you get a chance you could send me some?

It's just started to rain here and from the window I can see the cows waiting, all huddled together at the gate ready for milking. Maybe I should try writing poetry; just looking at that scene makes me feel full of life's simple beauty.

With fond regards,

Anne xx

3rd February, 1990

Dear Neil,

Just a quick note to say that if you wanted to come for Alex's party but didn't fancy staying at the farmhouse you could always stay here – we're a bit more civilized here, plus there's a spare bed and of course one of us will be driving back after the party. So.

See you on the tenth I hope,

Anne xx

By the way if you want me to meet you at the station or anything you can ring the pub and leave a message.

10th February, 1990

Dear Neil,

What a shame you missed the party. Alex said you had to work on a magazine or something? That's really tough having to work weekends. Still, you didn't miss much. The party was going fine until some of the rugby boys from the university turned up and started singing and chanting loud enough to drown the music. We left early (mainly because Gretchen and Liz felt really uncomfortable in the face of so much male arrogance – they are gay, by the way) which was lucky as the police turned up shortly after and a few people got busted – at least that's what I heard.

Well, just because you missed the party you mustn't think there isn't still the offer of a place to stay. The cottage we've got is in a nice quiet little valley near Llanilar, very near the river. It's a beautiful spot and very inspiring so if you just want somewhere to get away from it all and write you'd be very welcome. There's five of us here – Gretchen, Liz, Pete, Sue and me of course – but there's always room in the living room (and a spare mattress). You could use my room in the evenings if you needed somewhere private to write.

love Anne xxx

28th February, 1990

Dear Neil,

It was wonderful to get your card; I was beginning to feel like a bit of a nuisance. I really liked the picture on the front. Is the South Bank Centre where you work? Gosh, it's brilliant that you're off to India in a few days – send me a postcard won't you. You're so lucky to be able to travel alone. It's really difficult for a woman to do that, you know – dangerous. I do envy you, I really do. Maybe if I saved enough money I could join you there – that would be really cool wouldn't it? It's a shame you don't have an address in India or that you won't know how long you'll be there or where you'll be when you get back. I'd hate to lose touch again. I'll probably be at the same address for some time so don't hesitate to get in touch – even if you're dusty footed and broke on your return. I could easily put you up or feed you or whatever.

So have a wonderful trip, I'll think of you,
with love,
Anne xxx

16th September, 1990

Dear Neil,

The most amazing thing happened the other day (which is why I'm writing) I was flicking through a magazine and I found a poem by you. The funny thing was, I was in the bookshop not thinking about much, just browsing, you know. When for some reason I thought about you, I sort of had this vision of you in a dusty landscape wearing Indian costume and writing in a little notebook, when before I knew it I was turning to the page in this magazine and there was your name. Some coincidence isn't it?

So I had to write, you know, to say hello and also give you my new address. (Things turned nasty at the cottage and as the lease was in Pete and Sue's names and they wanted it to themselves I had to move out.)

But that's in the past now and I've got myself a little bedsit in town, just until I find another cottage. We writers need to be close to nature, don't we.

If you fancy coming to visit you could always sleep on the floor or maybe Alex would put you up – thought I'm not sure if he's still around, I haven't heard from him in ages.

Love Anne

P.S. I thought your poem was wonderful. You really are so talented. I wish I could say more, but it's really hard to describe such beautiful words.

1st October, 1990

Dear Mr Evans,

I'm very sorry to have wasted your time, as you so rudely put it. I was not trying to pretend I knew you or ingratiate myself and I'm certainly not a 'poetry groupie'. I was under the impression that you were a good friend of mine with whom I have lost touch. Of course looking at the poem again, I can see you don't have half the talent he has in just his little finger.

Please do not, under any circumstances, write to me again – especially not on a postcard. I have never been so humiliated in my life.

Ms Moore

P.S. I'm really not interested in whether or not you've been to India and I'm not interested in Naturism either. You deliberately misunderstood what I meant about being close to nature. I think you are nothing but a dirty-minded, talentless and corrupt old man.

28th October, 1990

Dear Pete and Sue,

I thought it was high time we all got in touch again. I feel in some ways that maybe it should have been you two who would approach me, but as that obviously isn't going to happen I suppose it's up to me. I feel very sad that things had to end up the way they did and I think we all said and did things that we now regret (I know I do). Let's meet somewhere for a drink, it would be so nice to be friends again.

I enclose a cheque to pay for the damage to Pete's car, though I still maintain that it was an accident – I just don't know how those bricks got on my window ledge and I do think that he did park far too close to the house and I had said that before. Anyway I hope you are both well and happy and that I'll see you very soon. Oh yes, before I forget, there isn't any post for me at the cottage is there? It's just that a friend of mine is in the Far East and he did promise to write. If there is anything, I'd appreciate it if you could drop it in or maybe give it to me in person if we meet up for a drink?

With love and regret,

Anne

28th October, 1990

Dear Sir,

Enclosed are two of my poems, which I hope you will consider for submission to your wonderful magazine. The first, 'Triangular vortex of the soul in torment' is based on a walk through the woods and was (I admit) inspired by Dylan Thomas, though I think I have now found a style that is entirely my own. The second is perhaps a more simple work; in it I draw on my everyday experience as a barmaid to show life's utterly futile, fruitless fripperies in the face of war etc, etc.

It would mean so much to me if you would publish these because sometimes I feel that poetry is all I live and breath for. My favourite poets are Dylan Thomas, Leonard Cohen and Neil Michael Evans.

I place my fate in your hands,

Anne V Moore

P.S. If you wish to publish them but cannot afford to pay

me straight away, then I don't mind waiting a day or so.

P.P.S. I am not enclosing the stamped SAE, as I will be calling into your office next week to see what you think.

28th October, 1990

Hi Alex,

I thought I'd just drop you a letter to say 'Hi' as I haven't seen you for so long. I've moved out of the cottage now as I felt I needed some time alone to write. Pete and Sue really wanted me to stay but I think there are times when it's important to have one's own private space. For myself, personally I feel like I'm finding some direction in my life at last and hope to travel soon. I've always been drawn to the Far East and suspect that it may be my spiritual home.

I'll probably be getting some poems published soon so I'll send you copies of the magazine when that happens. In the meantime if you're ever passing do drop in, we could have a chat about old times.

With love and serendipity
Annie xxxxxx

P.S. Heard anything from Neil at all?

8th November, 1990

Dear Sue,

I really don't know what to say. I've done my best to be fair to you and Pete despite the fact that you threw me out without even caring if I had a roof over my head or not. I've tried to put that in the past and I think it was noble of me to make the gesture of goodwill in paying something towards the windscreen. I don't think that I should have to pay the whole cost and I knew nothing about the damaged paintwork – I suspect Pete did that himself when drunk – he always did drink too much.

I don't think it's fair either, that you expect me to pay the last three months' rent when you know it cost me a fortune to hire the van in order to move plus I had to pay two weeks rent in advance on this place. I can barely survive on what I earn and it breaks my heart that you can turn your backs on our friendship. Here's what C S Lewis had to say (he is a writer, but I doubt if you've heard of him).

Friendship is unnecessary, like philosophy, like art...
it has no survival value; rather it is one of
those things that gives value to survival

Goodbye forever,
Anne

14th December, 1990

Dear Alex,

Thanks for the invite to your party. I didn't realize that you were living in Lampeter now. You should have let me know. I'm going to come to the party, though would it be alright if I stayed the night as I don't have any transport? I thought I'd come down on the bus and bring a sleeping bag with me. Hope that's okay – I don't mind where I sleep, on the floor in your room or wherever would do me fine!!

See you,
Annie

30th December, 1990

Hi Alex,

Great party! It was a fine feeling to be back amongst the green green grass of home. Though I think right now I could only take it in small doses. India was superb, you ought to get off that fat English ass of yours and get down there among the people, eh?

Being back in old smoky and living the high life is just what I need right now. I'm being wined and dined by this film company. I do believe that they think I've got real talent!!! – though I am trying to keep myself grounded – honest.

Hope you make it up to London before the mice eat all your underwear.

Neil

By the way, who the hell was that Anne woman at your party? She's not the one who keeps writing to me, is she? Whatever you do, please don't give her my address. The last thing I'd want is her turning up at my door, especially if Melanie was in...

6th January, 1991

Dear Neil,

Well, I suppose you must be wondering who is writing to you from Aberystwyth. Unless, of course, you've already looked to see whose name is at the end. I'll save you the trouble – it's Anne. We last met at Alex's party remember? I was the girl in the Leonard Cohen T-Shirt? The one who used to work in the Farmer's Arms? It's great how we haven't lost touch isn't it? I'm coming up to London soon so I'll drop round.

With fond memories,
Anne xxxx

P.S. I'm sure you'll be glad to have someone to talk to who really understands poetry and life and India etc, etc. To tell the truth I think that fate is just pushing us together over and over. It's a strange world we live in, isn't it?

Frog Boy

When my brother was seventeen, after he'd been to see the Super Furry Animals play at the Cardiff Arena, he killed himself.

He'd been given free tickets on account of his handicap – he was born with webbed fingers – but they made him sit down the front with all the people in wheelchairs. The technical term for this is syndactyly, though we tended to never use any word to describe it in our family. It was just the thing my brother had.

I think Michael killed himself just after the concert because he saw, like a blinding flash of inspiration, that this was as good or as bad as it was ever going to get.

The thing my brother really hated people saying to him was 'Hey, I bet you're great at swimming!' New teachers and new doctors used to say it to him all the time and then they'd look really pleased with themselves, like they'd said something original and funny.

After he discovered Monty Python's *Life of Brian* he would sing to them in response, 'Always look on the bright side of life' in this high pitched sneery voice. But then they didn't get that he was being sarcastic, because somewhere in their heads they must have thought that people with disfigurements were always cheerful and not very bright.

This was what my brother said, anyway. He didn't say it to me, or to anyone we can find, but wrote it in his journal.

Nobody knew he kept a journal until after he died because it wasn't a proper diary or notebook that he wrote in.

He was good at art and as it turns out, terrible at swimming. He had all these really nice hard-backed sketchbooks, which my mother always bought for him, and in his bedroom he had a big, pickled beetroot jar that was stuffed full of pencils. All sorts of pencils; HB ones with the little nub of eraser at the end, and all the grades of lead from 5H, very hard, to 5B, very soft. Whenever he got a new sketchbook he'd always make a big show of doing a drawing on the first clean white page. He'd sit at the dining room table with his pencils and copy something from a magazine. Early on he favoured comic strips, then it was fighter planes and tanks, then musicians he liked: Joe Strummer, PJ Harvey, Kurt Cobain.

Then he started doing some drawings from life. First he drew Molly the cat who helpfully liked nothing better than to sleep on the rug in front of the fire. Then he drew our Dad who liked a snooze on a Sunday afternoon after lunch. Then he drew Mum who would only sit for him if he let her read her library book. She was reading *Valley of the Dolls* at the time and he sketched the book in with great care so that you could easily read the title. She wasn't pleased about that and insisted he erase that book and draw her reading something better. Mum had a degree in English Literature and, as she put it, that picture misrepresented her. Finally she had to bribe him to change the book, and he switched the Jacqueline Susann for *Politics, Gender and Genre: a Marxist-Feminist Reader*. He was a long time doing it and when he showed us I saw that he'd also altered the expression on her face. She'd looked happy and relaxed in the first version, but in the second she looked intense and gloomy like she wasn't enjoying the book at all.

He drew me last and I pretended to be reluctant about it, but I'd been waiting and hoping ever since he drew the cat. I would even go and sit somewhere in his view and try not to move in order to show him how easy it would be for him to draw me, but he never seem to notice me. Almost three years went by between the sketch of Molly and the one of me.

I was thirteen, almost fourteen when he finally sketched me and he made me pose in the hallway. I hated the drawing when I saw it because I thought he was making fun of me, but now I love it and can see how clever and perceptive and talented he was. It shows me full length and I'm standing very straight with my arms by my sides. My hands are sort of resting on my thighs with the fingers slightly splayed. I think this last element is very significant. He is showing my hands, unwebbed, unflawed, and perfect: unlike his.

It's an inherited flaw, that webbing of the fingers; some people say it's a throwback to when we lived in the sea. It can skip one, two or three or more generations. We've got one set of cousins where all three of them have it, and another set without a single webbed digit between them, and you can see that the webless cousins think that they are superior in some way. You can guess which set of cousins we always preferred to be around.

The thing is though, that even if you escape as I did, the gene is still inside you. You can live your perfect life, marry your perfect husband and then find yourself to be the parent of some little web-fingered baby. Which is not to say that there isn't perfection even in those tiny webbed fingers and toes. The imperfection comes from somewhere else, and that's what is cruel.

After he died, my mother was too upset to even go into his room, so my father and I went up there on a Saturday morning and stayed there working at it pretty much all the time until Sunday evening. We were supposedly sorting through his things, in order to get rid of a lot of it, but what we were really doing was trying to find out who he was, why he'd done it.

My father got it into his head that my brother had been bullied, badgered, blackmailed. He was concentrating on my brother's clothes and he was searching carefully through all the pockets and whatever he found there; used bus tickets, sweet wrappers, receipts, crumpled tissues he put in a pile on the top of my brother's dresser.

We didn't talk much at first, but my father named stuff under his breath as he picked up each item.

'Socks,' he'd say, 'Wranglers, Levis, trainers.' Then, 'Ticket for *Pulp Fiction*. I didn't know he'd seen that.'

'Yeah,' I'd said, thinking about how I'd wanted to go, but couldn't pass for eighteen. My brother had a trick for getting into X-certificate films, for being served with beer; at the moment of the cashier's hesitation, he'd thrust his hand at them splay fingered, coins sliding on the palm, and after that they had trouble meeting him eye to eye and so he'd get what he wanted.

My brother's tricks – those were what made us feel he was all right. That and his insistence that he didn't want the operation.

They can do wonders these days – snip snip and you're perfect. But first of all my mother wouldn't let them do it – some weird notion she had about the developing child and trauma and rejection theory. He was supposed to make the decision when he was older. But he wouldn't do it, and then whenever our parents or his doctors or teachers or whoever brought up the idea of the operation he would somehow make them feel that he was okay and the problem was theirs.

'You think I'm a freak!' he'd yell. 'You think I'm ugly.'

'No, no, no,' they'd say, 'it's not that. It's not us – it's other people. It's ignorant people and look, you'd have that much more movement in your hands, you could do so much more....'

But there was nothing my brother couldn't do, apart from swimming.

'You can't bear to look at me, can you?' he'd say then, in a whisper that could break your heart.

It shouldn't have taken my father and me so long to sort through Michael's belongings, but both of us were possessed by a kind of torpor. We trudged from one side of the room to the other, as if we wore shackles on our feet. We lifted everything delicately, with great care, as if even disturbing a speck of dust might destroy our chances of finding the real Michael.

We were also trying to be as quiet as possible, so that Mum couldn't hear us. She knew what we were doing, she had suggested it, but we felt that her hearing anything would set her off on one of those weeklong crying jags again.

I had the job of sorting through Michael's books. I had to keep any that had inscriptions in, the ones that I or my parents or aunts or uncles had given him for birthdays or Christmas.

'Christmas 1998, Uncle Bob and Auntie Beryl', 'To our wonderful son on his thirteenth birthday! Mum and Dad'. We had always understood that not keeping books like those would be sacrilegious; like destroying family photos, like killing love itself.

So instead of just giving all the books to the church jumble collection, I had to look in each one for messages. My father also insisted that I fan open the pages of each book and give it a good shake.

By five on Saturday I had gone through all the books, and my dad decided that was enough for one day.

Over supper while Mum was in the kitchen, Dad told

me about a friend of his who had died when they were about twelve. The friend had fallen from cliffs while collecting seagull's eggs and when the family had cleared up his things they found that one of his books had a hollowed-out centre and inside was a stash of money. A lot of money for a boy from an ordinary working family in that day and age. My father told me the exact amount so you could see how important this memory was to him: 'Seven pounds, twelve and sixpence halfpenny.'

After he said that, he breathed in sharply, 'I didn't know what it was to lose someone. Oh God.' Then he got up and hurried from the room. I think he went upstairs to cry alone, because despite everything, my dad didn't think a man should cry and he wanted to hide it. But I heard him anyway, faint and pitiful; broken high-pitched sounds that I didn't think a grown man could make.

The next morning we continued with our work; the plan was to be done by Monday so that Dad could take the boxes to Mrs Harding at the church hall.

Dad gave me the job of looking under Michael's bed because of his bad back. It was there that I found my brother's sketchbooks. I lifted them out and laid them on his bed, then sat on the floor to sort through them. The first one I opened had the drawing of Mum reading the textbook. It was some years since I'd seen the sketch and along the way I suppose I'd got more sophisticated about drawing and this was not as good as I remembered. I thought, I could do one as good as this. Then as soon as I'd thought that, I felt ashamed of myself, because I was judging him and that wasn't allowed.

'Dad,' I said and I held the sketchpad aloft displaying the drawing, 'remember this?'

'Ah, you'd better keep that, maybe Mum would want to have it framed or something.'

Mum had wanted to have it framed long ago, that and the drawings of Molly and me and Dad. But my brother had said he didn't want to tear the page out just yet and he kind of hinted that these drawings might one day wind up as Christmas presents, but they never did and we all seemed to forget about them.

I turned the page idly, expecting more drawings, but the next sheet was blank. I turned another page and found that this one had been used, but not for sketching; instead it was filled with writing. The top line started straight enough, but as it went down the page, the writing began to tilt towards the bottom-right corner. My writing tended to do the same when I tried to work on unlined paper so for one moment I thought that this was something I'd written, but so long ago that I'd forgotten. When I read the first words however, I had no doubt of their author.

Monday. School. Sausages, mash and gravy. Peas. Semolina pudding. Maths, tech drawing, athletics, woodwork, French, English – Beerwolf. I'm going to kick Neil Jenkins' head in. Me and Dan and Lee waited for Jenksie by the south gate but he chickened out.

Tuesday. School. Maths, chem, history, German, cricket, double art – drew shoes. Geog. Mince, carrots, mash. Rice pudding with plum jam. Nick and Neil Jenkins are wankers....

So it went on for four pages, which covered a time period of about six months and was for the most part a record of school dinners. Nick and Neil Jenkins were twin brothers who were as obnoxious as they were handsome, and clearly they had made my brother the butt of their jokes. It seemed that they were in the habit of calling Michael Frog Boy and that was why my brother seemed to put a lot of effort into laying in wait for them after school.

It did seem to confirm my father's suspicions, and yet there was a sort of cheerfulness to the diary entries that made me feel that my brother was partly enjoying this warring game with the Jenkins twins.

Although undated, I guessed that these diary entries must be three or four years old.

I knew that I should have told my father about this find, but something stopped me. Partly this was fear about my father's reaction; I neither wanted to hear those man whimpers, nor see him rage. I knew him to be capable of both and so like a sensible Pandora I wanted to keep the lid on this box of horrors. Or at least keep them to myself until each ragged line of my brother's life was unravelled.

I sighed aloud, which was a habit of mine when I was troubled. I could do nothing to stop it as it was done without thought and was never meant as a form of communication.

'I know,' Dad said, 'it's hard. Want a break? Tea?'

We went downstairs and affected cheerfulness for Mum's sake, but I think it might have seemed as phoney as the bad actor that bounds through the French windows and says in plummy tones, 'Anyone for tennis?'

My mother had said that the last thing she wanted was

a shrine up there. She'd seen films where people kept rooms the same for years and years after the occupant had died and she thought it was creepy. 'I don't want to turn into Mrs Danvers,' was one thing she said, and we knew what she meant, because we'd all seen that film, *Rebecca*. At the same time we each felt that we were betraying Michael, but as my dad said, 'Keeping his smelly trainers isn't going to bring him back.'

Lunch was cold ham, boiled potatoes and peas and my dad said, 'Mmm, delicious,' and Mum lifted one cynical eyebrow, because we all knew she didn't give a damn about nice meals anymore.

I made an excuse to run back upstairs, 'I'm going to get my book.' I got the sketchpads – seven of them altogether – and stuck them in the wardrobe in my room. Dad had said that I could have anything of my brother's that I wanted and I'd already had his geometry set which was better than mine and also all his scary novels: *Cujo* and *The Midwich Cuckoos* and *The Shining*. I tried to kid myself that these diaries would also fall under that largesse, but knew at the same time that they didn't, or why else was I sneaking around?

I went back down and propped up *The Shining* between my dinner plate and the fruit bowl.

'Oh, don't read that,' Mum said.

'Why?'

'Oh, it's upsetting,' she said and I didn't know whether she meant it was upsetting for her or me. Or whether she felt that all those gory books had done something to my brother.

'It's good,' I said and she dropped the subject.

By evening we had done our work and in the hall we'd put the nine or ten boxes that held the last memories of my brother. I wondered about who'd buy the stuff, whether I'd see poor boys from school wearing his clothes and how that would feel and whether they'd know. And if they'd come after me because of it, threatening to beat me up. Calling me Frog Girl. It felt so selfish to be thinking about that when my brother was dead.

That evening I went to my room and ripped from the sketchpad all drawings he'd done of us and gave them to Dad. In the last book he'd done some drawings of frogs and underneath he'd scrawled, 'Use your eyes' which was less curious than it seemed. I had the same art teacher and it was something that was always being said, over and over, until actually the words lost their meaning.

On the next page there was writing and there was a title MURDER and he'd done it in red biro so it was meant to look like dripping blood. Underneath he'd written 'He must die!' I closed the book as soon as I read that and ran downstairs, slipping on the loose carpet near the bottom and almost falling.

Mum came out from the kitchen wiping her hands on her apron.

'Julie,' she said 'are you alright, sweetie?'

I'd wrenched my wrist as I'd grabbed hold of the banister to stop my fall and now I cupped it in my other hand.

'Ouch,' I said, and then I sat on the bottom step nursing my hurt arm. Mum just watched me. I had taken to shrugging off her hugs, claiming it was babyish. I could see she wanted to put her arms around me and kiss it better, and I could remember how once that was all I wanted too; the comforting arms, the soft engulfing lavender-perfumed body of my mother.

'Ouch,' I said, but the pain was ebbing away. I studied my wrist, willing it to bruise and swell, hoping for some visible sign of injury.

Then I looked at Mum and I asked her a question which I did not even know I needed an answer for. Not until it was spoken anyway.

'Mum,' I said, 'why do we hurt?'

She sat on the step next to me and we gazed off in different directions and did not touch.

'I don't know darling, I really don't. I wish we didn't, because then...'

Her voice trailed off and she seemed to be thinking very hard. I waited. Finally she spoke again.

'Maybe we hurt so that we remember we are alive.'

I knew that wasn't the answer, because hurt is what kills you, but I didn't say that; instead I put my arms around her and kissed her cheek because at last I could. I was old enough.

The Inheritance

Liam's nickname at school had been Perry. It wasn't until years later that he began to understand the significance of the name. Which was this: Perry Como – homo. He tried to laugh it off, by remembering what his Mammy had told him about nicknames being signs of affection, only given to popular children. Yet he felt discomforted by it and sensed, beneath the laughter, thinly-veiled hatred.

He knew that despite his undiluted accent, the teasing had nothing to do with being Irish. After all, his elder brother was at the same school and his nickname was Paddy – and crude and predictable as that was, it didn't carry the malice and menace of the hated Perry.

Liam was shockingly good-looking. While he tended to avoid mirrors; hating the particulars of his features and colouring, women of all ages and types seemed to respond to him with approbation. Girls his own age would blush and giggle when he was near, and women in their twenties and thirties would appraise him with frank, devouring gazes. Older women eyed him wistfully, as if remembering something undiluted and poignant from back before he was even born.

Liam, it was said, had inherited his gleaming blue-black hair and big dark eyes from his great aunt Caitlin. She, he was sick of hearing, had been a famous beauty – the toast of Dublin, and Yeats himself was supposed to have written a poem dedicated to her sparkling eyes. But there was a rise, a climax and a fall to the tales of great aunt Caitlin. After the talk of the lightness of her dancing step, the delicacy of her little white hands, there was always a deep sigh and a shaking of heads, then: 'Twas a pity. A blessed pity.' And then, 'Poor Caitlin....' After this someone, usually his grandfather, would pipe up with a warning note in his voice and repeat some cliché about 'beauty paying its price' and 'pride coming before a fall', or in a gentler mood, his words half lost in a whisper, he'd say how only the good died young.

Liam and the other children had learned that no amount of questioning or excited clamouring would extract the answer to their pleas of 'What happened?' and 'How did she die?' So great aunt Caitlin held onto her secrets and took them with her into the muddy waters of the Liffey where, it was hinted, she'd chosen to take her last brackish and watery gasps of life.

Liam discovered that the gift of her inherited beauty tainted with him the curse of her tragedy. He wished he'd taken after Uncle Sean with his walleye and freckled face and bad breath. Or even Auntie Roisin with her face so flat and round and her nose so small and upturned, Liam's dad said she looked like someone who'd been whacked full on in the kisser with a shovel.

Liam looked, more than anything, like he didn't belong to that family. Both his mammy and his daddy, and all his brothers and sisters, had sandy or reddish hair and all had eyes that were quite pale and watery, in varying shades of blue and green. They each had fair eyebrows and lashes which gave them a distinctive look; a sort of lack of expression. Liam, in contrast, looked distinctly Mediterranean, as if some angel in a moment of perverse humour had stolen a sallow-skinned baby from its cot in Padua or Tuscany and deposited him in County Mayo. Was there some unfortunate red-haired youth, Liam wondered, growing up in the ancient alleys and back streets of Italy, forever cursing his freckles and blue eyes?

Perhaps because of how he looked, Liam was always being mistaken for someone artistic; a poet or a painter. But this was not the case. He wasn't even one of those people with the yearning to create or perform, but who sadly, possessed none of the talent. Rather, Liam had an analytical mind, one full of theories, measurements, comparisons, equations, blueprints and percentage graphs. Thinking about anything that could be measured in grams and kilograms, joules or watts, farads or therms, made the world feel good and solid under his feet, while art and poetry made him feel lost and lightheaded.

He could not see the point, in the scribbled or

painstakingly-penned notes and poems he often found in his desk or sports bag. They would be decorated with flowers, and hearts punctured by little arrows and were sometimes anonymous and sometimes signed. They came from Shelley or Julie or Tracy or Cathy. Why, he wondered, as he disposed of yet another note, did all the girls who swore to love him forever have names that ended in 'y'.

Sometimes there'd be a gift along with the note. Back home when he'd been eleven or twelve he'd been given toffees or fruit and once, inexplicably, a Biggles book. But now, just as the shape and look of these girls had changed – with their stockings and high tottering heels and hairspray and cone-like breasts – the gifts also changed. He'd been given a miniature of cherry brandy which was far too sweet (although he'd drunk it anyway), a small lump of cannabis wrapped in tin foil that he hadn't recognized and which he'd thrown in the bin after giving it a tentative lick to see if it was a toffee, and a David Cassidy single which he'd recycled by giving it to his sister for her tenth birthday.

Lizzie Morris, who was reputed to have slept with half of the Rolling Stones as well as David Bowie and Marc Bolan, gave him a pair of knickers. They were made from a slippery black nylon material and had details in fraying red lace. The elastic had gone in one leg.

The message that accompanied the last item was as lurid as the gift and the next day, Lizzie had pressed herself up against him in the queue outside the language laboratory. As he registered the two hard points of her breasts where they met his shoulder blades, she whispered for him to sit up the back next to her. He didn't take up her offer and on the way out at the end of the lesson she pushed roughly past him, and red-faced, hissed 'You're fucking dead, McCabe!' He shivered, but it was a shiver of relief. Lizzie's love, he was sure, would have been as crude and violent as her hatred.

Yet everything seemed to change after that. People suddenly began avoiding him – some subtly, some obviously; overplaying the way they moved away from him, saying loudly 'I'm *not* sitting there!' Others; his gentler, but not very brave friends were taunted away, afraid of persecution through contamination. And the name he got called changed. It was no longer the vaguely unsettling Perry (which he'd come to think might have something to do with his Mediterranean appearance); now it was the blunt and indisputable: queer, fairy, poofter, bum boy, pansy.

To make matters worse Lizzie got herself a new boyfriend – a skinhead who called himself Kurt because he thought the name sounded strong and Germanic. Liam had once seen him spit in the face of a little Asian girl who couldn't have been more than twelve. Liam had seen it and done nothing, but then there must have been thirty or forty kids in the playground that day that saw it and did nothing. All of them did nothing, but shrink away and think themselves lucky that they hadn't received Kurt's special attentions that day.

For a year Liam practised the uncertain art of invisibility and at the same time he tried to come to terms with what he told himself was 'his difference'. If he was what they said he was, then for him it went by another name, but what name that was he didn't know.

One Saturday when he was eighteen, Liam was in town getting some shopping for his mother. Carrying three bags of shopping, he'd wandered down a back road in search of a second-hand record shop he'd heard about, when out of the past came a voice that was unmistakable.

'Oi! Perry!'

It was a girl's voice, husky and over-loud – Lizzie's voice. He stopped and turned. Lizzie was half standing, half leaning, draped over Kurt and surrounded by six or seven other young men who struck postures managing to combine both boredom and menace. Lizzie, who'd left school over a year before, looked much older and scrawnier than he'd remembered. He noticed that she had bleached her hair white blonde to match Kurt's and had cut it so that it was no more than a quarter of an inch over her skull, except for a short and curiously wispy fringe that fell over her forehead.

'Oi. Come here.' Lizzie smiled as she said it, while Kurt gazed off into the distance, grinning at some private joke.

Liam, after briefly considering flight with his precious cargo of Sunday joint and other essentials weighing him down, walked cautiously over. It had rained earlier. Although the sun was now out, the sky was still filled with ominous slate grey clouds and there were a few shoppers about.

'Got any money to lend us?' said Lizzie in a tone that verged on sweetness.

Liam hesitated – maybe if he just gave them a few shillings with the pretence of it being a 'loan' that would satisfy them. He reached into his pocket and took out all the money he had, a one-pound note and some change. Awkwardly, holding all three bags on one arm, he selected the coppers and offered them to Lizzie.

In the meantime, the group had drawn closer – someone, he sensed, as Lizzie reached for the proffered money, was moving around behind him.

'Come on, mate,' said Kurt, and while the skinhead still gazed aimlessly into the distance, Liam saw that he was openly and dispassionately kneading one of Lizzie's breasts. And she was letting him, as if it were her knee or shoulder.

Liam was watching Kurt's hand as one might watch an unusual animal in its cage, when several things seemed to happen at once. Something pushed him hard on the back of his head, while a foot, which must have been aimed at his genitals, struck his inner thigh. The bags were ripped from his arm, horrifying him more than the sudden violence.

He stood in dazed silence while they began to inspect the shopping. The onions and carrots and leeks they discarded by lobbing them, Frisbee-like into the road. The shoulder of lamb, his father's stout and his sister's medicine they set aside. Then they came to the packet of sanitary towels his mother had insisted he get for her. These received special attention. The packet was ripped open and the contents waved in his face like terrible flags.

'Jam rags!'

'I said he was a frigging woman didn't I!'

Later Liam would vaguely remember saying or beginning to say 'Okay, a joke's a joke...' but maybe that was something he'd dreamed or overheard when he was unconscious in the hospital. He did remember rain; big thunder drops that splashed onto one side of his face, and something hard and cold pressed against his other cheek. And he remembered looking with numb fascination at his lower leg that seemed to be bending the wrong way, as if it didn't belong to him at all. He remembered too, the hospital; the urgent crash of equipment, the hurried voices.

After he recovered, his good looks miraculously unimpaired, he found that his parents had changed towards him. Suddenly he was their 'darling boy'. They treated him as if he were made of china and at the merest touch might break. They were always talking, for those few days while he sat propped in the armchair in the front parlour with an eiderdown over him, about what was best for him. And what was best for him, they decided, was to go home.

'But I am home!' said Liam.

'No, no! Back home to Ireland,' they soothed. 'You can stay with your Auntie, Mary Coogan in Dublin.'

Liam's parents had come to the conclusion – perhaps they had no wish to see it any other way – that he'd been attacked because he was Irish. It had, it was true, been only a month since the big bomb went off in Guilford and in England they all felt a chill wind in its wake.

Liam protested half-heartedly; apart from the family what was there to keep him in London? And besides it was Dublin that was being proposed – not Limerick or Tipperary.

Mary was Liam's mother's cousin and was a year or so older then her. She had been an only child and after a brief marriage had been widowed. She had gone back to live with her parents and after their deaths she'd stayed on in the family home, a large three-storey town house. She was considered the last of the Coogan clan and thus the holder of the family's stories and treasures, such as these were.

Mary had sold off the three lower floors of the house and now occupied what had once been the servants' quarters in the attic. Because of this arrangement most of the good furniture was crammed into the few rooms she still occupied, giving the place an atmosphere of Victorian clutter.

Liam was to sleep on a camp bed in the living room – a situation that forced him into greater contact with Mary than he'd envisaged, but Mary, despite appearances, was a pleasant, witty woman with an easygoing spirit, keen to entertain her recuperating guest. She fell only a little short of spoiling him.

Mary brought him a cup of tea every morning at nine. He'd wake to the faint clatter of the kettle being put on. He listened as the cup and spoon rattled on the saucer as these were borne towards the room in which he lay. Mary would be half singing, half humming I Could have Danced All Night or Molly Malone or The Sally Gardens. He wondered if she sang just for him or if all these years she had filled the attic with her lonely soprano and sweet sad songs.

During her first week Mary had suggested she show Liam around the city so that he wouldn't get lost when he walked these streets alone. But somehow they fell into a pattern of spending each day together.

Into the room she would come and after setting down his cup of tea she would open the curtains and comment on the weather. 'Tis a grand day for a walk in the park.' And so after breakfast, off the two of them would go. In the evenings they would listen to the radio and while Mary picked up her knitting and began yet another patchwork square, Liam would pick up his book on Keynes' economic theories and open it at the first page.

Every day for a month he sat with this same book open on his lap and every day he would fail to read more than the first paragraph. It wasn't that Mary's distraction was unwelcome or irritating; that would have been easy to cope with. No, he loved to hear her talk, to listen to her stories. She kept him entranced with the wealth and depth of her knowledge, with her frankness and bright laughter. It was as if she'd stored up all the unspoken conversations of her youth and now they all came rushing out at once.

Liam, who had always been conservative and neat in his appearance, suddenly no longer found the time to go to the barber's once a month. His hair grew and within months it fell over his shoulders in black rippling cascades. Mary said he looked like a wild Irish Prince.

One winter evening, when Liam had long given up lifting an unread book onto his knees, he and Mary were sitting in the firelight when she suddenly stopped her knitting and said, 'I should show you something – why have I not before?' She disappeared into her bedroom then returned, carrying a small trunk, and set it down on the floor in front of the fire.

Together they knelt on the hearthrug and Liam reached forward to open the box, but Mary stopped him. 'Wait,' she said and hurried into the kitchen, coming back seconds later with a very dusty bottle of whiskey and two clean tumblers. She poured each of them a small measure then settled down beside him again.

With great ceremony Mary opened the trunk. Liam peered inside, intrigued by its contents and the importance bestowed on what looked to him like a collection of old clothes. Mary dug down deep as if she had memorized the exact position of the thing she sought. She drew out an album bound in black leather with the word 'photographs' tooled in gold on the lower right hand corner.

Liam drew closer. They sat, their backs resting on the settee, with the book held between them. Liam briefly saw stiff Edwardian figures posed between potted palms or Greek columns as Mary turned the pages, searching for the particular picture she wanted to show him.

'Ah ha, here it is!' she said finally. 'Now who do you think that is?'

Liam found himself staring at a black and white photograph, six by eight inches. It showed a handsome young man, his head turned artfully at the neck, so that he was presented three-quarter face to the viewer. One black and liquid eye looked mournfully out, while the other was half lost in the shadow of a tilted trilby. The shirt he wore was white and crisply starched; the collar stiff and formal.

'Who is he?' asked Liam, feeling a strange mixture of desire and recognition.

'Wait,' said Mary turning the page, 'look there!'

Liam didn't understand the triumph in her voice – it didn't answer his question. Here was another photograph, but this one was of a young woman. The pose was similar, yet everything here was softer; feminized. Her eyes, though equally dark, seemed beguiling, and a coy smile played at the edges of her lips. Her hair fell in dark glistening waves over her slim white neck and danced across the pale lace of her collar.

'Are they related?' asked Liam, turning the page to and fro for comparison.

'You could say that.'

'Well, come on Mary – don't be a tease – tell me, who are they?'

Mary looked delighted. She took a sip of whiskey and smiled. 'That,' she said with evident pleasure at the trick, '*that* is your great aunt Caitlin.'

Liam was about to say 'and the young man?' but the penny dropped before the words had reached his lips. 'Jesus!' he said, and then snatched the album to take a closer look, 'that's amazing.'

Liam vaguely remembered hearing other family stories about Aunt Caitlin; something about her 'being in need of a good fella' and how she possessed an unfortunate independence of spirit. How after she died the family was horrified to find that she'd left all her money to a woman who wasn't even a relative, but a mere lodger.

'Ah, but there's more. Go and look in the mirror,'

Mary said, delighted with her game, '*and then* look at the pictures.'

Obediently, Liam stood before the mirror, and with the album resting half on his belly and half on his right arm, looked first at himself, then at the young man and woman. Then he looked again. And again; until all the faces became one.

One that was beautiful; but was neither totally male nor female. It was perhaps only a trick with mirrors and light, and yet for the young man on one side of the looking glass it was more than that – a melding of souls, an inheritance of difference.

She Speaks Kölsch

Herz Bar was small; small in the way bars used to be around the outskirts of his native town in Ontario, but he was a long way from home now.

The place was down at heel, but as spick and span as it was possible to be. Its owner, Christopher Herz died all of eighteen years ago and first his widow ran the bar, then, after she too died, his beautiful daughter Astrid took over.

Neither Herz, nor his wife, nor Astrid (now aged twenty-eight and ethereally beautiful with pale moon-kissed skin and long, naturally blonde, naturally curly hair) had any illusions about the kind of clientele the bar attracted. Those women of the night, so many of them *melaten* or dead blondes with sallow skin and dark eyebrows. With eyes that while they might 'do' beguiling well enough, would very soon after turn again to shadows.

And the men who came there? They were working men drawn to the city for better paid jobs, or men on the run from small town loneliness, to hunker down at the bar as if it were a second home with their elbows propped on the counter, and a pale Kölsch beer between their calloused paws in a straight slim glass only five or six inches high.

The first night the Canadian had wandered in there he didn't notice anything out of the ordinary. The place was small and he had seen a lot of bars in a lot of different cities. He rather favoured the shabby over the genteel, the basic to the ones with frills and chrome chairs or neon light or someone's idea of abstract art on the wall, and customers so cool that the beer or champagne or cocktails never got warm, maybe not even by the time they were pissed out into the black enamel designer toilets.

Not that he resented the people in the cool bars. Quite the contrary really; he pitied them, as there, in the bruising strobe or neon lights, with the bilious rainbow-coloured drinks and the crash and scream of what passed for music, no one ever really talked. It was only the appearance of talk, and what was said was only the hollow strutting of pose and fear and scorn.

The Canadian was a rep for a pulp mill in his hometown. The job was dull but his spiel was polished, if over-rehearsed, and the work did afford him the opportunity for endless travel to countries he might otherwise have never seen.

He had a taste for the novels of Dashiell Hammett and Raymond Chandler, and always carried a yellowing copy of one or the other at the bottom of his overnight bag like his own personal and idiosyncratic St Christopher. He rarely read them any more though; it was more the case that he needed the books' presence as an antidote to the Gideon bible, which lay like a black heart in the bedside cabinet of every hotel room he'd ever passed through.

October of 2004 found him in Cologne at the tail end of yet another office supply trade fair. His German-speaking colleague had left two days earlier after a family crisis, and so the Canadian was washed up among the gas lift chairs and super Pentium processors and paperclip bores without much sense of purpose and little hope of new contracts. His bosses had wanted him to explain the improvements made at the mill recently, but his phrase book wasn't much use when he wanted to translate 'conversion of an idle recovery boiler into a low-odour bubbling fluidized bed boiler' into German.

Not that it mattered to him, he didn't work to commission. It was just one of those things, and going back home early would only make more expense for the company, so he kicked his heels back and let his mind and body drift out of focus in the last warm days of the Rhineland's Indian summer.

He'd been married once; long ago now it seemed, to his college sweetheart Brigitte; a pretty girl from Quebec who made great martinis, but cried too much. She cried over injured puppies and sick children and sad films, and things he said and did without thinking. So. That was then. He'd been alone, without quite meaning to for sixteen – no, seventeen years.

He thought of time as abstract, as meaningless. Considered himself quite a philosopher really, which translated as someone who could see through all the bullshit – whatever the bullshit was: religion, politics, vapid consumerism, art, drug culture – sex even. And certainly and resoundingly, romantic love. What he believed in was solid ground. Here, now, and then death. No more, no less.

Or at least that's how it was when he stepped out of his hotel on Fredrikstrasse and turned the corner into Johannastrasse where halfway along, with road works blocking the street and pavement in front of it and in sight of the twin spires of the cathedral as they poked two fingers at God, he stumbled upon Bar Herz.

It was dark inside the bar, but not so dark that his eyes needed more than a second or two to adjust. He hesitated at the threshold for perhaps a moment and quickly took it all in. The bar itself was long and narrow, made from a dark plain wood, and ran down along the left hand wall. To his right was a row of diminutive booths, with low upholstered benches and a glass Coca Cola ashtray on each tabletop. Three out of the five booths were occupied, most of the clientele choosing instead to gather along the length of the bar, either seated on the high wooden stools or lolling comfortably against its sturdy flanks. Like a row of piglets, he thought later, though he meant nothing by it, only seeing the comforts of drinking companionably together, the calming bliss of the beer, the bar like the long body of a sow happy to give suck.

Nobody paid much attention to him; only the merest glance registered his presence. Another stranger. That's all he was, another stranger amongst many.

He moved forward, found a stool, sat and turned his gaze to the person behind the bar. She was down the other end, just five or six paces away and he was thirsty and hoping that this wasn't the sort of place where he might become invisible. He kept his eyes on her, waiting for her to see him. Her hair was long and blonde, and danced against her slim back with loose fluid curls. She wore tight-fitting jeans and had the narrow hips of a boy. He noticed this, but in a disinterested way; the way one sees a tree on the way to work, and it's just a tree, nothing special. Ah, but then, then comes spring and the tree is a magnolia bursting into life with its branches covered by a hundred vivid pink flowers. And that's how it was when she turned towards him and he saw her face; her face which was that of a glowing Botticelli angel. She came to him then, seemingly gliding from one end of the bar to the other, with an expression that was so subtle you would almost not even call it an expression.

She lifted her eyebrows, gazed at him, exuding the kind of untroubled patience such as one sees in paintings of Saint Agatha even as her body is maimed, or Saint Catherine up on the spiked wheel. Or Saint Ursula; blank, beguiling and limpid in Memling's painting of her death in Cologne.

She takes his breath away, obliterates language; any and all language from his mind and all he can do is raise one finger like John the Baptist pointing heavenward.

'Kölsch?' she says with a voice that manages to be both businesslike and gentle.

He nods and watches as she fills the slender glass from the tap, then marks one pencil stroke on the beer mat before she is finished with him and busy elsewhere.

His mood is suddenly transformed. It is as if he's been asleep for the last ten or maybe twenty years. Asleep like some old rat-eaten Kodiak bear snuffling in its cave buried deep within the earth, under the snow, under life itself, hibernating until she brought spring.

He swallows the drink in three swigs. The diminutive glass seems to hold a mere quarter of a pint of beer, but no one there seems to be drinking from anything larger. Not the grizzly stevedore with his thatch of black hair spilling from his shirt collar, nor the Cologne cowboy with his James Dean quiff and narrow eyes and pack of Lucky Strikes, nor his friend who likes to drum on the edge of the bar, extemporizing and fantasizing and becoming by turns Elvis, then Buddy, then Duane, regardless of his receding hairline, his growing paunch.

He wants to stare at the barmaid, but is aware that despite the way the bar is in some ways like a stage with an audience gathered around all facing inwards, it would be impolite to do so. He gazes off, towards the window at the front through which he can see the buildings opposite, but this barely keeps his attention for more than a minute. Then he watches the people at that end of the bar. There are three men and a woman and he assumes that they are a group of friends, until the woman, seemingly tiring of their company moves to the other end of the bar where she fixes herself in the shadow of the cowboy and his rock'n'roll friend.

Then the Botticelli angel is standing in front of him with her face serene and astonishing in its beauty.

'*Bier*?' she asks, indicating his empty glass and he nods, grateful for her attention. She fills the glass and marks his beer mat with another single stroke. She doesn't smile. She seems to smile at no one, as if smiling would be letting down her guard.

But then the Canadian isn't much for smiling either – never was. He finds that formal politeness, rigid handshakes, correct address; sir, madam and crisp business procedure all do well enough without grinning and backslapping.

Put another way, he wants to sell paper pulp, they want to buy it, and any deviation from that essential deal is not only unnecessary, but also phony. This barmaid, he notes, is drawn with the same blueprint as him; she pulls glasses of pale yellow nectar, she marks the beer mats with the tab, runs a cloth along the Formica surface of the bar, and she takes the money, but that is it. But suddenly he is taken with the notion that he would do anything, anything to make her smile.

The light in the bar takes on a rosy appearance from the last of the sun. Maybe it's the sort of evening, the sort of showy sunset that should be enjoyed from a beer garden overlooking the Rhine, or at a chic café table near the Dom, but right now, in this stripped-bare place with the angel administering to him, that merest hint of a reddish glow is enough.

Another Kölsch, another pencil stroke on the beer mat. A small man, Mediterranean-looking, but probably Turkish does a strange limbo-like dance in the narrow space between the bar stools and the booths. Palms raised for balance; for effect, and knees bent low to support a body that arches backwards, the man shimmies lustily and shuffles forward as he does. His dance seems to be performed for one person in particular; she is a tiny bit of a woman, with the prepubescent build of a healthy Canadian eleven year old. Only her face belies the slight body, for there are grey smudges of shadow beneath her eyes, and her skin has the pallor of a pickled herring.

The dancing man's finale is an almost impossible feat of gymnastic skill in the narrow space that barely separates the bar stools from the booths; but suddenly he flips himself over in a backward somersault, making a perfect, piston-legged landing only inches from the Canadian's stool.

It could be taken as a challenge; a way of unsettling the stranger amongst them, but it is done so lightheartedly and with such uncaring panache, that the Canadian sees that it is done only for the act itself.

The Canadian glances at the barmaid to see if the somersaulting man has raised a smile on her face, but she is busy pulling another beer and she is impassive, closed off, private.

He makes a decision; one more beer then he is out of there, but somehow he cannot quite shift himself and soon his beer mat is decorated with three more pencil lines and, improbably, it feels as if he will never leave and will live out the rest of his days here, die here.

He has lost track of time, and now it is properly dark outside, but there is something comforting about the glossy blackness that presses against the window. He checks his watch, estimates that he's been here on this stool for almost two hours and he still hasn't seen the angel behind the bar either smile or frown.

He gets up and makes his way to the toilet at the back. There are a pair of black plastic symbols on the outer door that leads to both the men's and women's lavatories – the *Damen* is identified by her short crinoline skirt, whilst the *Herren* is starkly unadorned.

Beyond that door there is a minuscule space the size of an old-fashioned British phone box. The door to the gents' is straight ahead, while the ladies' is to the left. He pushes the gents' door open to find a space that is only marginally bigger, with just one urinal, one washbasin, and one stall. It's unoccupied and he unzips himself, positions himself at the urinal and gazes at what is probably a health warning about Venereal Disease that is stuck in a metal frame on the wall at eye level. It's in German of course – in modern script – though he thinks the old gothic style of typography would probably be more arresting.

He washes his hands and dries them under the hot air device, catching a glimpse of his bleary face in the smeared mirror over the sink. He's still here then, he thinks, still ugly. Though of course, he's not really ugly at all, just sick of that same face rising to meet him day after day with that same faint scar cutting across the outer corner of his left eye, glancing over his cheek and ending with a complicated flourish at the left side of his mouth.

While he is standing there, contemplating the scar which is pale and silver and all in all a good, well-healed one, he hears the outer door open and close, and footsteps moving about in the small space beyond. He moves away from his door because it opens inward and he doesn't want to get thumped by it if someone comes through with a heavy push. He waits, then hears another door open and close, and then voices. A man's voice, deep and questioning saying one of the few German words he knows.

'*Entschuldigung*?' the man says. Excuse me.

There is the briefest pause in which the person being addressed might have responded with just an answering look. Then he heard the man ask another question, a single word that the Canadian also knows the English meaning of, '*Arbeit*?' 'Work?' or perhaps in this context 'working?'

Next he hears a woman's voice; almost a whisper, conspiratorial, 'Ja'.

Yes.

More words follow. Words that he cannot translate, except that he understands the heat of them, the sly expectation of pleasure in the man's tone. A bargain is being struck, but one that doesn't involve shipments of wood pulp, or contracts: this one is done for cash and will be completed within the hour.

He hears the outer door open and slam shut, and then he too leaves the cramped space and re-enters the bar. His eyes go first to his angel, to see if she is still there with her patient Botticelli face, her small elegant hands working the beer pump. Working. *Arbeit*.

And she *is* there, as is his place at the counter, with his two inches of Kölsch waiting and the pencil marks on the beer mat indicating what is owed, what he has consumed.

He takes his seat, swallows the last of his beer and raises his empty glass so that she knows he is ready. Swiftly, smoothly she produces another beer, slides the beer mat across the bar, scores another mark on it. The pencil lines are like the scratches on the wall of a prison, each one marking a passage of time. Or maybe they are like the notches on a bedpost that keep a record of every sexual conquest, every new lover.

The word 'whore' pops into his mind, and he looks at the angel again with her guileless face, her mouth that wouldn't melt butter.

He's feeling bolder now, glances about the small interior with renewed interest. One of the three women who were there before has gone and so has the dirty little trucker with his stubbly chin and his black fingernails and his perfume of engine oil and sweat.

The small woman, the one with the child's body, is sitting in one of the booths with a bald man in a red and white FC Koln shirt. The man's got a body like a barrel; a barrel topped by man breasts that droop sluggishly onto the belly. He's leaning against the back of the bench like some ancient potentate; a god-like man with a little slave girl humbling herself before him, laughing at his unfunny jokes.

The other woman is near the front door. Her hair is short, stiff, an unnatural shade of platinum; *melaten*. He notices a sort of earnestness about her stance; what he'd taken before as awkwardness he sees now as the alertness of a body attuned to work.

Another beer slips easily down his throat. He looks again at his empty glass and it seems to take on a new significance, for it apes the girth and height of an erect, though admittedly modest penis.

He is maybe getting a little drunk; but it is a sort of smooth drunkenness, a descent into one shade of madness, where his thoughts still flow in an analytical and intellectual way but wander off to places which his sober mind would not dare approach. He is still staring at the penis glass when his angel suddenly wraps her pale, well-manicured hand around it and this act quite naturally takes on the look of some bizarre and arcane pornography.

He breathes out, long and slow and nods, yes, he wants more, but it isn't really beer he wants, it's her. She fills the glass, reaches for the beer mat with her pencil poised to mark his seventh or eighth drink and he, without thinking, without any plan, catches her hand in his.

He addresses her in his native tongue, which she doesn't understand, and so her answer is only a gentle resistance to his touch. He smiles as she stares at him but she does not smile back, instead her eyes move uncertainly to the Cologne cowboy at the end of the bar.

Remembering himself, the Canadian gently releases her hand and struggles to find his few clumsy German words.

'*Entschuldigung, bitte,*' he says, then, after licking his lips as his mouth has become strangely dry, he manages to say, '*Was ist sie name?*'

She looks at the beer mat as if searching for the answer there. She does not want to say her name, or give him anything. She does not want to give anyone anything of hers. Not now anyway, not here. And so she looks at the row of pencil marks she has made and remembers the story of Ursula and how the saint came to Cologne on a pilgrimage with eleven virgins and how all of them were massacred. How later scholars somehow misread the eleven as eleven thousand. How silly that is she thinks, and almost laughs to think of such a miscalculation of scale.

'*Bitte*,' he says and she looks at his face and notices for the first time how lonely he looks, how lost and half-drunk, and she leans forward a fraction and whispers the name she has just this moment christened herself with.

'*Ursula*,' she says, '*mein name ist Ursula.*'

He lifts his newly-filled glass, raises it higher in salute of her and says her name, filling his mouth with her, before drowning it in Kölsch.

Now that she has told him her name, his mind is spinning off like a mad thing, like a pinball whizzing here and there, bouncing off cushions, setting off lights, bells, buzzers, defying gravity, and whenever the ball threatens to drain out of play, sets the flippers in action by remembering how she leaned forward and almost smiling, barely keeping a straight face, whispered her name to him.

He does not notice that the Cologne cowboy has moved a little closer, then a little closer again, until the two men are almost elbow-to-elbow. He hasn't noticed either, the subtle and secret eye contact his angel has been making with the cowboy, the way she has been saying with her eyes, 'Watch out, this foreigner is odd.'

He does not notice because he is too busy imagining himself to be in love.

And yet even while he is soaring away on that idea; on that vision of himself and the angel Ursula flying off on invisible wings like something Marc Chagall might have painted in hot shades of red and green and blue, he is also thinking lustfully of her, of how he will possess her, squeeze her flesh until she bruises, bite her neck until she cries out, push himself into her and into her until there is no him left, only a profound sensation of pleasure bursting like a firework.

Lust and love. He is aware of how easy it is to confuse the two, just as it is easy to mistake an angel for a whore or vice versa. Or at least he is usually aware of that, but tonight he's mad. Tonight he's a moon-eyed Canadian lost in an unknown city with one too many of those devilish beers inside him.

And yet, if drink is the life spring of this sudden flood of emotion, it could also be the thing that drowned it.

She was avoiding him now, he thought. Floating around at the edges of the bar, avoiding his eyes, avoiding the sight of his empty glass, as if to see it would be to confront his vast emptiness. And she has seen enough emptiness in her short lifetime to fill a book. Except that such a book would have no words in it, only page after page of virgin paper and nothingness.

She guesses that the stranger is North American, though from where exactly, she can't tell, but the usual assumption is the US. She also guesses that he is here on a business trip and that he has come to this bar to find a woman. It does not occur to her that anyone, even a foreigner would wander into this bar not knowing what sort of place it was. Everyone knows that at night near the railway station there are working girls of every kind and description. One only has to ask a taxi driver or perhaps a hotel porter. Or failing that one can just open one's eyes.

Can't he see, she thinks ruefully, that she is not for sale? That there is a difference between her and the girls who are here tonight: Ebba and Rayya, and little Ecaterina – or Cat as everyone calls the tiny Rumanian girl?

Emotions rage through the barmaid's mind: pity, anger, sorrow, even a small smudge of joy as this fool is gazing at her so dolefully she might almost believe that he really loved her. None of this shows on her face, she wears serenity like a mask. It's a trick she acquired as a child when the other kids found out about her mother's line of work.

She has seen that the foreigner's glass is empty, but she has also seen how Gerlach is paying too much attention to what the stranger is doing. Gerlach, who for some strange reason, decided that she is his girlfriend, which she isn't and never would be. Gerlach with his mean eyes and his 1950s quiff that makes him smell of hairspray, a smell she associates with her dead grandmother. And yes sometimes she has been glad to let him walk her home, but he should not then think that he could throw his arm around her shoulders and let it hang there like a dead weight. Nor that he can stumble through her apartment door with her without any invitation, which happened once. Nor that he can kiss her, or certainly not in the way he once tried to. She had offered him her cheek in a sisterly way, as he had earlier said that all girls needed big brothers to protect them. He had told her about his own younger sister, how she was a pretty little thing but had some mental incapacity; something about how the birth had gone wrong and she was starved of oxygen. The story had made her see him in a new light and so when she offered him her cheek outside the lift that had led to her apartment, she might have allowed him one chaste kiss on the lips. That would have made her begin to love him. Perhaps. But instead he had bunched his fingers into the hair at the back of her neck and forced his tongue between her teeth.

For a while he had given up on her and was seeing Cat. He was paying Cat of course, but not so much that Cat could give up the game even if she had wanted to. That had ended badly one night back in April. Cat had a customer who was a regular. A wealthy banker called Doctor Heinz. His taste was for young girls and you could always tell when Cat was expecting him because away would go the high-heeled boots and the lipstick and eyeliner and padded bra, and in would come the braided hair and the pink t-shirt with the heart motif. Without her boots it was always such a shock to see just how tiny Ecaterina was: just four feet and ten inches.

Gerlach had followed Cat and Doctor Heinz when they left the bar. Maybe if she had taken him to a hotel nothing untoward would have happened, but instead they had gone to a children's playground. At first the Doctor had just pushed Cat to and fro on the swing, then he'd watched her climb to the top of the slide, watched from the bottom of the ladder so he could see the white cotton pants he insisted she wear. After that they went hand in hand to the far corner where there was a little wooden playhouse. Cat said afterwards that all the good old doctor wanted was to look. He never touched and there was never any sex. She also said that it was better that she did this for him, than that he should go prowling around for real little girls.

Gerlach had watched what happened in the playground and by the time Cat and the doctor emerged from the little house, he was in a state of crazy self-righteous fury. He strode towards them and Cat tried to stand in front of the doctor to protect him, but Gerlach pushed her aside. He knocked the man down and then began to kick him.

Cat said that the strangest thing was that it was all so quiet. None of them screamed or shouted. She could hear the sounds of scuffling feet on the wood chips and the laboured breathing of both men, and the noise of Gerlach's boots as they struck their target over and over. She heard, she said, the sound of bones cracking. 'But the blood was grey,' she said another time, 'like in that *Psycho* film, when the blood goes down the drain, and you don't see how red it is?'

The doctor survived. There was a story in the paper two days later about how the much-respected doctor had been set upon by thieves who forced him at gunpoint into the playground where they beat and robbed him. 'There were three or four of them,' the doctor was quoted as saying, and Gerlach found that very funny. So much so that he carried the newspaper cutting around in his wallet for a few weeks until Cat secretly stole, then burnt it.

Gerlach frightened Astrid, although she was sure he would never hurt her. Not unless he found a legitimate reason to do so. There were devils everywhere, Astrid thought. Devils one knew: like Gerlach, and devils one didn't know: like this stranger when he grabbed her hand and wouldn't let it go, but who now only seemed lost. Lost and sad and drunk. She regretted the eye contact she had made with Gerlach earlier. The panic she had allowed to flash across her face, which she could not now undo. And there was Gerlach, sitting almost elbow-to-elbow with the foreigner and watching his every move and waiting.

The stranger lifts his empty glass higher and angles his chin and cranes his neck and tries to catch her eye. He does not understand why she doesn't notice him and so he knocks on the bar's surface as one would knock on a door. Calls out 'Hey!' because *entschuldigung* is too much of a mouthful.

He does not notice that the man next to him has pushed his stool back and is now half standing, half leaning on the seat as if preparing himself for action of some sort.

His angel notices. She sees everything, even things she would rather not see.

It would be so much easier if the stranger actually spoke German. Or if she spoke more than a handful of words in English. Then she could ask him to leave, warn him of the impending danger.

Instead she goes to him and takes the empty glass away and fills a clean one for him. She fixes her gaze on Gerlach and shakes her head. Gerlach understands and settles on his stool once more, but as he wants to show her what a big man he is, he cracks the knuckles of one hand in the other and breathes out noisily through his nostrils.

The door to the bar opens and Ebba comes back in alone; her hair is slightly damp as if she's just come in from the rain.

She asks for a Coca Cola and Astrid gets it for her and says, 'Is it raining?'

Ebba leans forward, an angry glint in her eyes, and whispers, 'I had to take a bloody shower cos the bastard came in my hair, even though I told him not to.'

Astrid does not really want to know this, and Ebba is the worst for this sort of kiss and tell. In Ebba's view she has nothing to be ashamed of, she is only in the business so that she can make a good life for her twin sons. It is the men, she says, that should be ashamed.

But Ebba has a good heart, and she is a loyal friend. It occurs to Astrid that perhaps Ebba can help her with the foreigner and get him out of harm's way. She goes down to the far end of the bar and gestures for Ebba to follow. This is not an out of the ordinary event, as Astrid often has cause to talk to one or other of the girls in private, either because they have misbehaved in some way or because customers have left messages for the girls with Astrid.

Ebba listens to what Astrid has to say and glances at first at the foreigner and then Gerlach. She nods slowly, understanding the dilemma, and then she whispers in

Astrid's ear; outlines a foolproof plan. The two young women look at each other steadily, Ebba lifts her eyebrows as if to say 'well, shall we?' and Astrid bites her lower lip, then gives her assent with a bob of her head. She has a tip jar behind the cash register and now she reaches into it and extracts two twenty euro notes, folds these haphazardly in a small square and after first checking to see that she is unobserved, presses it into Ebba's palm.

The Canadian feels very tired suddenly; he glances at his watch and sees that it is almost eleven o'clock. He shouldn't feel this tired, though maybe the drink, and the tensions of another city and his stupid disappointed heart are conspiring to exhaust him.

He is still watching *his* girl. What surprises him is that she seems to run the entire bar single-handed. But then as she is so serious and determined and thorough, she does not need anyone else. Unlike him, who without his German-speaking contact has completely given up on all thoughts of doing any deals at the show tomorrow. He is aware that this tendency of his to give up; to throw his hands in the air in defeat at the slightest setback is perhaps why he has been overlooked for promotion again and again and again. That and his failed marriage, which shouldn't matter but does. There are all those dinner parties his bosses and colleagues throw, which he has been invited to less and less over the years. The wives of all those men do not like him for some reason, though he tries to be civil, brings a bottle of whisky and, when he remembers, flowers for the hostess. He showers compliments on the food, even when it is not very good. Smiles at their children, though they never seem to warm to him, not in the way they do with his colleague, Bruce, who they greet like a long lost uncle and who seems to know as if by magic just what sort of toy to bring for them, or when and how to make them laugh.

The Canadian sips his beer slowly now, meditatively. He will go when he has finished it. Must not, cannot order any more, and so because he doesn't really want to leave, he's making this drink last.

A woman comes and sits beside him, and he smells her before he really sees her. She has a fresh country smell like apples. She has rested her right hand on the bar near her drink, and with her left she is absent-mindedly tracing her fingers over her forearm near the sensitive spot inside the elbow. Her face is turned away from him, but he is certain it is the woman whom he overheard in the toilets, the whore. He could have her, he thinks, and that wouldn't be such a bad thing, would it? He could close his eyes and imagine another face; the sort of face you wouldn't want to miss even for as long as it takes to blink.

He assumes that this is the pick up, that she will try to catch his eye, ask him to buy her a drink and then a price and a place will be negotiated.

He'd regret it afterwards, but he knows he could leave the regret behind, leave it in Cologne, let it fall from him as the plane soared over the city and arced north to his homeland.

His angel is once more keeping her distance, she is at the far end of the bar, talking with one of the other whores. She has barely acknowledged his presence this entire night, and so he wonders why he ever imagined for one second that anything could have happened between them. He might as well have fallen for a woman in a painting or a statue or a movie. Whereas.

Whereas here at his elbow, with her knees slightly parted and tilted in his direction, is the real thing. Or at least the available thing. He lets his eyes drop down and to his left. She is wearing a tight denim skirt that has risen up to mid thigh and her legs are bare and tanned, though they are not as slim or shapely as he would like, but they look strong and that is exciting to him. She is wearing some sort of tracksuit jacket that disguises the shape of her upper body, but it's zipped open just enough to reveal the single black shadowy line of her cleavage.

He catches the merest glimpse of her mouth and eyes before he tears his gaze away. It isn't that he doesn't want to take a good hard look at her face; it is rather that doing so would move things along and he is still uncertain about what he wants.

But then everything changes, and it seems as if choice is taken from his hands. The man next to him, the one with the 50's quiff is talking to the woman. He is talking to her across the Canadian, and his tone is rough and insulting, aggressive and loud.

The Canadian leans back in his stool, affecting an air of casualness that he does not really feel.

The woman answers the man in a tone that might be playful, might be challenging. They talk back and forth, and the man's tone becomes softer and the woman's more seductive.

The Canadian, from his awkward position catches sight of the angel and sees that she is watching what is happening, and he swears that for the first time he can see the merest flicker of a smile flash across her face. But it is like he is seeing something far off, something so brief and elusive that he can barely believe his eyes. Like the northern lights perhaps, but even more tantalizingly beautiful and temporary.

Then he senses movement on either side of him. Movement that is swift and certain and businesslike. The man and the woman have got down off their stools, she is tugging at the hem of her denim skirt, straightening it, making herself decent, and the man is downing his drink, then calling out *wiedersehen!* and shrugging on his dirty suede jacket.

Once they have gone, the bar seems suddenly quieter and also more relaxed. Maybe, the Canadian thinks, he could just have one more drink for the road, one for the narrow escape from sin he has just had, because, one minute longer, or even one second longer and he'd have met the whore eye to eye, and then? Something to regret, perhaps. Certainly something that should be forgotten; eviscerated from the mind, like newsprint from recycled pulp.

And the last drink is another excuse to draw his angel to him, to make her attend to him; to be his for as long as it took for her to fill the small glass, and lift her pencil to mark another debt on the beer mat. A mark that he will never know is also the mark that turned his life this way instead of that. As is often the way, there is no way of knowing. Not really.

A Memory Game

Pauli is in London again, but contrary as ever, he misses the sea. He is homesick, but stubborn. He is trying his luck here, as others have done before him; he imagines his time in the English capitol as a short spell in Babylon, done not because of any enforced servitude, but in order to make enough money to buy a small plot of land in his native land; with a vineyard, an olive grove or lemon orchard. After London, he would clean the city's contamination from his hands with his forefather's red soil.

He'd first come to London for a short visit with his stepbrother, Ari. Ari was sixteen years older than him. Then, Ari had seemed to him to represent the pinnacle of adulthood and assured masculinity, but now Pauli realized that Ari had been barely out of his teens and was still wet behind the ears, and what had seemed manly confidence was merely bossy or patronizing arrogance. Ari had been asked to come to London for an interview at the London University and he had been bribed into taking Pauli with him, so that their newly-wedded respective parents could have a belated honeymoon on Lake Garda in Northern Italy.

Pauli, being a mere child, and a rather trusting and particularly guileless one at that, had viewed the second marriage of his mother and the prospect of a new father as something that could only be good for him, just as spinach was good for him, or sums. With hindsight, he could now see that perhaps the marriage had not been as welcome for his stepbrothers, as it had for him. That they might have resented the sudden acquisition of a new mother, when they had spent a good seven years running slightly wild in a home devoid of any womanly presence, or feminine niceties.

However, considering the circumstances of the trip, Ari had been a kind and indulgent older stepbrother; he had bought Pauli books and crayons, and even a wind-up toy train with a single track that they laid out on the floor of the hotel. Ari had shown him how to turn the key in the train's base and warned him against over winding it, and Pauli had treasured the toy to the point where he almost felt afraid to play with it, though conflictingly he was also aware that not playing with it at all would look bad, and he wanted desperately to win the approval of this tall stranger who was suddenly part of his family.

One day, Ari had announced they were going to see something called *Piccadilly Circus*, but when they arrived, there wasn't any circus at all, and Pauli had begun to snivel, then finally; unable to help himself, because he didn't understand the deception, to sob. Ari had pointed to the statue of Cupid on the little island surrounded by cars and red buses, and told him that if he didn't stop crying it would suddenly come to life and shoot him in the bum and then wouldn't he be sorry?

There were steps all around the statue and people were sitting there in little huddles. They were young people mostly, and a lot of them had khaki or grey-coloured rucksacks with them. Pauli, even at that young age had a sort of disdain for authority, which quietly triumphed in the outward signs of non-conformity, (perhaps this was why he liked the circus and clowns in particular) and so he viewed the gathered tourists with a sort of baleful envy. He liked the way they slouched on the stone steps, took frowning puffs of cigarettes between cupped fingers, or kissed furiously and openly.

It was the middle of the day and while he noticed the many complicated neon lights on the buildings above them, he was unimpressed, as was Ari.

'We'll come back later, when it's dark. Then you'll see.'

Ari had shown him a photograph of the same place in their guidebook. The photo had been taken at night and all the brightly-coloured advertising signs shone out of the dense blackness like the baubles in Ali Baba's cave. It looked like the sort of place where there *would* be a circus; where there would be all sorts of pleasures and excitements for a boy of six. Toys and candies and funfair rides and dancing horses – that sort of thing. Not this grey, petrol-smelling, choked-up city of busy adults who regarded children, especially tourist's children, as nuisances one had to briskly manoeuvre around.

When Pauli had finally stopped crying, they had wandered around the area between Charing Cross Road and Piccadilly Circus looking for somewhere good to eat. Ari had attempted to translate the names of the food on offer in the various pubs and restaurants, but he was invariably stumped by names like *Toad in the Hole* and *Cottage Pie*, and had to concentrate on the simplest of items; like the ubiquitous *chips*. He'd asked Pauli if he liked this or that sort of food, but Pauli's only answer was only a confused shrug of his narrow shoulders.

Finally, on finding an establishment that seemed to suit their requirements, Ari guided Pauli inside and found them a table. Pauli could remember the smells of the dark interior vividly; there was a strong beery smell, and also a visible fug of cigarette smoke; enough of it to make his eyes sting. But there was also the aroma of frying onions, which smelled, consolingly, like home.

Ari had helped him off with his coat and pulled the low copper-covered table a little closer, and had begun reading the menu card, when a man came from behind the bar and told them they had to leave.

Ari had tried to ask, in stammering broken English, what they had done. But he could not understand what the man said in response, though he understood well enough the man's arm raised dramatically to shoulder height as he pointed towards the exit, and his look of detached, but undisguised irritation.

182

Ari had said a bad word to the man in their native tongue, which Pauli marveled at as he had rarely heard it used in such a direct and pointed way. The moment was confusing and a little frightening, but then it was quickly over, and they were outside on the cold grey street again. Ari was red in the face; he had the scorched look of a child who has just been punished, and was about to stalk off angrily, dragging Pauli along with him, when a woman came out of the pub and stopped him. She addressed Ari in rapid English, and then seeing that he did not understand, repeated it slowly.

Ari shook his head. 'No English,' he said.

The woman pointed at Pauli and said it again, then realizing she needed to change tack, she simplified her words, 'No kids. None *bambino*,' and jerked her thumb back at the doorway to the pub.

Ari looked relieved, he smiled and relaxed his shoulders, then pointed at Pauli, 'Ah, no child,' and in imitation of her gesture, he thumbed the air in the direction of the pub.

She laughed, pointed again at Pauli, waggled the same finger to and fro, and then pointed at the pub. The more she did it, the more Ari copied her and the more they both laughed. Pauli had stood solemnly watching them. Waiting for whatever would happen next.

The woman folded her arms then, and leaned on the white pillar to her left. She adjusted her feet, bent one knee so that all her weight was on one leg. Pauli thought that she looked very pretty; that her hair was the same bright yellow shade as that of the fairy princesses in his picture books, or like that of the foreigners who came to his town for their holidays; the Germans and the Scandinavians who swam in their sea and lay on their beaches. Except that this woman's skin was as white as the pillar she was leaning against and her lips were dark red like salami and around her eyes were the dark smoky shadows of smudged mascara.

'Okay,' Ari said, 'okay.' And Pauli thought that was going to be goodbye, but neither Ari nor the woman made any moves, but just stood there smiling at one another as if they were sharing some private joke.

Pauli broke the silence by reminding Ari that he was hungry, and as if to appeal to the beautiful blonde lady, he rubbed his tummy and looked puppy-dog sad. Well, it used to work with his aunties, but then perhaps England was different.

The lady, when she finally noticed him, laughed, which rather wounded him, but then she ruffled his hair and turned to Ari and began to communicate by using some impromptu sign language. She pointed at her open mouth, then mimed eating; flinging invisible food into her mouth with an invisible knife and fork. Then she made a face that seemed to pose a question and waved her flat palms to the sky as if she were bouncing it gently up and down.

Ari nodded and patted his belly in response.

The woman nodded back, said 'Okay,' and then beckoned them to follow her. Ari fell in beside her. Pauli had wanted to walk next to Ari, and hold his hand as they had done for most of the last two days, but the lane they had turned into was narrow and crowded and it was all he could do to follow in his brother's wake.

From the lane they turned into a road which was only slightly wider, but was filled with market stalls, and brimmed with both people and noise. Pauli might have been frightened, but the street market reminded him of home. There was something very comforting about the sight of this everyday commerce, the stalls of potatoes, tomatoes and bread, and the handwritten signs with their prices.

After a few yards they came to a little Italian café with steamed up windows, and signs advertising Coca Cola and milk. Pauli followed the two adults in and when they were all seated, quietly gazed about him. He rested his hand on the tabletop and discovered that it felt surprisingly clammy and sticky.

It was strange that he should remember the feeling of the sticky table so vividly, while so many other, and perhaps much more important, events during that trip had been thoroughly erased from his memory. Like what happened after the café, or what he actually ate there, or where the lady with the yellow hair went, and who the other lady – the one in the hotel room, had come from. Or maybe there hadn't been two different women, perhaps his immature self had been forced to separate the two, so that his first impression of the pretty, kind lady could remain, whatever her actions later. Perhaps the events happened on different days. On different trips even, as he was sure that Ari had once said that the two of them came to London more than once.

'And I *always* had to take little Pauli,' he'd said only last summer, and he'd followed the remark with a wink, as if to emphasize the necessary curtailment of his younger self's pleasures, but also to make it seem as if it didn't matter.

But then a wink can also mark a lie. And there had been a nasty dispute going on between the two sides of the family ever since Pauli's stepmother had died suddenly the previous April.

'Do you remember,' Pauli had asked, pronouncing each word carefully so he would be sure it found its target, 'that blonde woman?'

Ari's smile had quickly faded. They were sitting in their uncle's garden, at the long table under the grape arbour. Ari's wife was there, and their father and uncles, and Ari's two little girls; both of them in pretty white dresses with ribbons in their hair.

Ari had reached across the table to pick up the wine and poured it into his glass, filling it to the brim.

Seeing this, Ari's wife had sighed, and said, 'So I should drive then?' and Ari, by way of answer had taken a long swig of the wine, and wiped the back of his hand against his mouth as if sealing it shut.

Pauli knew that he should drop the subject, but something, perhaps that last gesture, drove him on.

'When we were in London, when I was six, I remember there was this woman...' Ari wouldn't look at him, but gazed towards the end of the garden where the citrus trees were. 'Who was she?' Pauli said, 'I've always wondered about that.'

Ari didn't answer him, and instead he addressed his daughters, 'Hey girls, you want to pick some oranges? Ask Papa nicely, and he'll let you.'

In chorus the two children squeaked their willingness to both pick the fruit and ask nicely.

Their Papa waved his hands in the air to signify his consent, and the girls ran off towards the trees.

'Not too many,' Ari's wife called.

'The thing is,' Pauli said, 'I've always wondered who she was, and...'

Ari turned on him, he was angry now, his face was flushed, his mouth a sneer.

'The thing is, little brother,' he said, 'the thing is, *you* were a kid. The thing is *you* still believed in Saint Nicholas and the tooth fairy. The thing is you're still a damn kid, okay?' Everyone had turned to look at Ari as these words poured out of him, souring the atmosphere, tainting the remains of the feast.

There was a moment afterwards when no one spoke, no one moved and the air was very still, and each person heard the rhythmic tinny throb of cicada as if it were a new sound that they had never heard before. Then, as if on cue, one of Ari's girls – the youngest, prettiest one – screamed and Ari was on his feet and headed in their direction as if pursued by demons.

But by the time he reached them, the scream had turned into a laugh. Then as one of the girls spotted her father, she had called out, 'Daddy!' with such exquisite and unrestrained joy that hearing it one could almost cry.

Everyone turned to look at Pauli, each of them with eyes wide open in astonishment. What was he supposed to do now? He had no child to hurry towards, no fatherly duty to distract him. He was, as Ari had rightly said, just a kid. And like a kid he stood up with deliberate violence, causing the chair to scrape along the paving slabs and almost fall. And he cursed loudly, as if the vile taboo words could prove his status amongst the grown ups.

Ari's wife called out his name in a pleading singsong 'Paul-i!' but he ignored it and stalked into the house through the kitchen door. Once inside he stopped and blinked, letting his eyes adjust to the dimmer light, and then, momentarily at least, let himself cry. But they were men's tears; staunched almost before they had begun, unlike the tears he'd cried so frequently when he was a child.

He remembered crying in that hotel room in London, and the way the toy train had looked after it was broken; the way the wheels had folded inwards on one side where the metal rod was bent. And he remembered what had caused the toy to get broken; how in the middle of the night he'd got up to use the bathroom and found it locked, but then when the door was finally opened, he'd seen not just his brother, but that strange woman too. How, just before she left, the woman had gestured to his brother; rubbing her thumb around and around on the pads of her first two fingers.

At this Ari had looked at first confused, then frightened, and he had tried to manoeuvre the woman from the room, but she shook herself free and in the scuffle she somehow stepped back onto Pauli's new train, crushing it.

London hadn't changed much, or at least not those parts he still remembered. The statue of Eros was the same, except that the traffic no longer poured endlessly around it; part of the area was pedestrianised – but all the winding streets, and alleys and lanes, and the market in Berwick Street – those were much the same.

And Pauli was now a man of twenty-four, two or three years older than Ari had been then. And he was lonely and would perhaps have liked the company of a younger brother; it would have been a good excuse to do all those things that were perhaps unnecessary extravagances, trips to Madame Tussauds, or the Tower of London.

In some ways he felt *too* free. He could go where he wanted, drink as much as he liked, stay in bed all day, scratch, fart, wank, belch and no one cared. But there was no one to talk to. No one to listen. No one to touch.

Pauli understood more now about Ari and the woman. *She* must have been a whore. But Ari? What of him? Had he known what she was, or was he almost as innocent and ignorant as six-year-old Pauli? Ari had looked shocked that night long ago, had shaken his head when the woman rubbed her fingers, wanting money. 'The bloody fool,' Pauli thought, 'the dumb country bumpkin.'

That was why he would not talk about it last summer; it wasn't guilt, but embarrassment at his own stupidity and lack of guile.

Pauli had sat on the steps beneath Eros, the stone felt cold and hard under him. His trousers were light cotton ones, better designed for the southern heat than this northern city. As soon as he started to make more money, he'd buy new slacks, and a warmer coat, and he'd find a better place to live: his current room, though warm, stank of the fried food from the café two floors down. He wanted somewhere nice, somewhere with a couple of rooms, so that he could entertain, have friends back. Except that there were no friends just yet, and perhaps, given his circumstances, might never be.

Well, maybe one friend would be enough. Just one. A woman. Someone to love. Someone to love him. Someone he could trust. Who would be like the other matching half of his soul. Who needed him.

He thought about the woman with the yellow hair; wondered how old she had been then, how old she was now. And he found himself looking around for her even though he knew the idea was preposterous. Her hair must have been dyed, and her face was made up in such a way that what one remembered were discreet elements; the black-rimmed eyes, the scarlet mouth, rather than a recognizable face in its entirety.

And what if he found her? It was an absurd proposal, a theory only, but one that he momentarily wished to pursue if only as a sort of test of his moral fibre. If he found her, then what? Fuck her, as he supposed Ari had done all those years ago? Press her against the tiled wall of a cheap hotel bathroom; give it to her silently, guiltily while a small child slept beyond the bolted door?

Or perhaps only speak to her. Ask her questions. Ask whether Ari had known what she was? But no, more than that, he wanted to ask about himself, to discover whether she was surprised at the sort of man he'd become?

Or whether she could have predicted it, had seen enough of those raw tourists to know it all; its end and its beginning.

The Ghosts of
the Old Year

I won't admit to loneliness. That is too much of a sign of weakness, a sign of defeat. I don't want pity, but I don't want this empty night pressing down on me.

The baby is asleep now and that leaves her absence; her silence in the room like a great hole. Remember the story of Jesus in the Garden. It was his last night of freedom, and the others – his friends – fell asleep. He couldn't sleep knowing what he knew, but they slept. I wonder what they dreamed that night, those ghosts of long ago.

My baby sleeps. She has no ghosts. She laughs at the pictures I have painted of my ghost. My ghost is a smiling woman. I keep the paintings hidden. They are my secret. They are all the same, these pictures. There was just one photograph to paint from. I found it in his wallet.

There, you see how I am; sly and jealous and full of rage. I can't help it, though. She has done this to me. So now I must work some evil on her. And so I paint her. I like to use wrong colours, to paint like Matisse, Rouault, Dufy, Derain. They called them the wild beasts and that suits me. That is how I feel. I give my ghost all her prettiness. I never take the baby plumpness from her cheeks, nor the brightness from her eyes nor do anything to mar her two perfect dimples. She must look as she looks in the photograph: beautiful, desirable, sweet. All I do is give her green skin or red eyes or black lips.

These are probably my best paintings. But no one will see them. I'll make sure of that. I keep the pictures in my wardrobe. Her face is pressed against the rough wood in the darkness and that way I am safe. That way she is in my power. I can take the memories in and out of the cupboard at will, give myself little doses of pain like medicine and try to forget.

I remember the time before as a golden age. I was happy. It's true that often he disappeared for hours, days, weeks even but I would sit with the baby happily suckling at my breast and feel content. Four months went by like that and I looked forward to Christmas like I hadn't for a long time. Since I was a child I suppose, when I was filled with all the longing for carol singing and chocolate and tangerines and the thrill of waking up on Christmas morning to find at my feet the heavy weight of one of my father's old socks filled to brimming with presents.

Now for the first time I was a mother and I could live it all over again for my child. I would make each Christmas a magic time with soft fairy lights and angels everywhere and the smell of pine. The dream was like a Christmas bauble, all shiny glass, brightly coloured, hollow, fragile.

He didn't come back. I waited up all Christmas Eve, telling myself that he was out there somewhere searching for a taxi, walking through the gone-to-bed streets of Swansea. What if there had been an accident and he lay dying? I saw myself, a brave and weeping widow with a baby in my arms at his graveside. I pushed the idea away and thought he must be drunk and how he'd turn up the next day, sorry and sweet, his arms filled with mistletoe and presents and love.

Christmas day passed like any other, except that the streets were empty, the shops and cafes closed and when I went out for a walk and looked at other people I saw in them perfect happiness. Their smiles and laughter loomed large and rosy, and I passed like a wraith away from them, a little match girl in my misery. I kept my eyes on the pavement ahead with my eyes following the grey slanting shadow-shape of a lone woman pushing a pram.

He was with her, of course. She had wiped me from his mind with one look and made him forget his daughter with her light dancing laughter. I blame her for everything. I blame her for her blue eyes and slow smile. I blame her for her soft breasts and the taut skin of her belly. I see the facade of her nineteen-year-old face and underneath it I sense only wickedness and cruelty.

I read the baby a fairy tale in which beauty is good and age and ugliness bad, and I curse the princess who could not sleep because of a pea beneath her mountain of mattresses and I curse all the princes who believe that she is the only true good woman in the world.

So I paint the nameless ghost in red and green and purple. Yellow eyes and vermilion teeth, black tongue and emerald skin. I paint her as the snow queen all wintry white and icy, with kisses that will freeze his heart and make him forget his little Gerda.

It was New Year's Eve when I found his jacket and hugged it to me wanting him, missing him, still fearful of the overturned car that may have killed him, the drink that made him sleep in the ditch until he died half frozen. I lay down on the bed and held it like I wanted to hold him and my hand found his wallet and I took it out and opened it. There inside was the photograph.

I handled the snapshot like a precious relic or a thing cursed. I set it on the table and sat on the other side of the room. Occasionally I'd get up and go and look at it again.

It was only a photograph. Only a smiling woman on a summer's day with a ribbon in her hair. Yet she became summer itself, and turned me into winter.

As the day wore on I began to avoid the table, walking in gradually wider circles around it, averting my eyes from the grinning succubus I had set free. I could not concentrate on anything except the photograph. I tried to read while the baby took her midday nap, but the words on the page were a useless jumble of ill-expressed sentiment that had no meaning. The smile of the succubus filled the room and stopped the clocks and pressed against my chest until I gasped for air.

It began to grow dark at two o'clock, I was not sure which one of us had pulled the sky down like a vast grey blanket heavy with snow, but the day was gone, the sun lost forever.

I wondered what I should do to exorcise this ghost. I could stub my cigarette out on her face, burn the photograph, tear it up, obliterate the smile, the ribbon in her hair, the summer dress. Slowly gouge out the blue eyes, cut the hair from her scalp, scratch through her with a pen, furiously criss-crossing her image until she was all gone, but she wouldn't be gone, she would merely become more elusive. To destroy her I had to know her. That was the secret.

The baby woke then and I opened my blouse and guided her mouth to my nipple and she sucked and patted the full milky flesh of my breast with her little hand and sighed her satisfied sighs. In the stillness my hurt took the shape of anger, my fear became revenge and I wondered if my raging thoughts would turn the milk sour and poison the child in my arms.

The night slipped away into sleep and my dreams were the dreams of the haunted. In the nightmare I went into the bedroom for what reason I cannot tell, and the ghost was there curled in his arms. That same smile from the photograph fixed on her lips for eternity. I found my hand suddenly tightening around a knife and I raised it high ready to strike, but as I watched she seemed to shrink and fade away until it was only the baby that slept against his warmth. I stopped my hand and as I did my daughter opened her eyes and seeing me began to cry and I awoke to the black confusion of night and the real sobbing of my child.

The next day I knew what I must do. I stretched and sized a canvas, taking more care with its taut surface that I had ever done before. Its whiteness seemed to draw me in, speaking of a peace and purity I had never before noticed. I was not afraid as I usually am, to make the first mark. It was not going to be a beautiful painting, one to hang in a gallery and sell, but one that would live with me, be right or wrong with me, and would perhaps eventually be destroyed by me.

The first painting took nearly two months to complete, I worked at it every chance I got. January passed like one long night. I don't remember seeing daylight but somehow the baby grew and I fed her and washed her and loved her. By mid February I was on my second canvas, I knew the woman's face well by then, so that the merest flick of my brush could indicate an eye, and it was her eye.

Now it is January again and there are thirteen paintings, each one more loose and vibrant than the last. They are my best work. They are as beautiful as the cobwebs on Miss Haversham's wedding cake and as flawless as the nails in Marley's coffin. The thirteenth will be the last. It is the perfect number. It is the number of Judas as he reaches forward in the garden to betray the man who hasn't slept.

Once I am certain that my daughter is sound asleep, I clear away her playthings, the beloved debris of the day, and bring out all the pictures. I prop them up around the room against the table, the playpen, the high chair, the settee, and I sit cross-legged on the rug with them circling me. I am a stone in a ring of bright flowers, blanched of colour, empty of feeling.

' I close my eyes. Open them again. This is my garden; these my paints, my colours, my light. I am not a stone, impassive, without art. I am a gardener, a god, and tomorrow is a new morning.

The Player

I suppose that some people might think it's a bit pretentious of me to stand by the window and play my violin. Malcolm said so after he arrived early one day to pick me up.

'Jesus,' he said 'what do you think people think.'

'I don't know,' I said 'and I really don't care.'

'Yeah well, you look like some right geek up there – showing off with your bloody violin and your wee prissy music stand.'

Malcolm's been a friend of mine now for nearly five years. We started out as lovers; but that only lasted two weeks, but somehow it was brief enough and painless enough for us to remain friends.

We have, admittedly, drifted apart when one or the other is seeing someone else. For example, when he was first living with Mona, I don't think I saw him for a whole year. Mona by name and moaner by nature is what I used to call her, as she was the one who elbowed me out, probably with the idea that the more isolated he was, the faster she could scoot him up the aisle to wedded bliss and babies and all that.

I knew her number was up when he started to drop into my workplace at 5.15 just as we were finishing for the day.

'Fancy a wee dram?' he'd say and I'd say something to the tune of 'Oh, are you sure Mona wouldn't mind?'

'Ach,' he'd say with a couldn't-care-less shrug of his shoulders.

Malcolm is from Glasgow and he's so thin you'd think you'd cut a lip if you dared to kiss his cheek. His hair is auburn, the sort a girl would kill for. Lately he's had it cut close to the bone, which suits him I think. And the other thing is, Mona the moaner hates it.

Malcolm used to make fun of my flat because it was so spartan. But I just can't bear clutter.

'You're a strange girl,' he'd say and that used to upset me, but only a little.

Now I feel like saying to him, 'Be careful what you wish for,' because of course, Mona is anything but spartan. There's her pig collection for one thing. Maybe he thought that was cute at first. Maybe then she had only the china pigs; no more than ten or twelve of them in a row on the window ledge of their new house. But now there are pigs everywhere. Prints of pigs on the walls. Pigs on the crockery. Stuffed toy pigs. Plastic squeaky pigs. A copulating pig clock in the kitchen that has the words Makin Bacon printed on it.

Last Wednesday when Malcolm and I went for a drink in the Prince of Wales, he was beside himself. The pub was busy and there was nowhere to sit, so we stood by the bar necking bottles of Stella.

'What's wrong?' I said.

He took a long swig, then brought the bottle down hard on the counter and sniggered a little. It was one of those sniggers that contains a sneer. Well, at least he was still able to laugh at himself, I thought.

'It's Mona's birthday next month.'

'Ah,' I said, feeling mildly surprised because I thought he was about to invite me to a party for her.

'She's told me what she wants for her present.'

'Oh, let me guess,' I said, 'it wouldn't be a pig of one sort or another would it?'

I'd helped him find a Christmas present for her just months ago. Which was an authentic oil painting. One of those naively-painted ones with a pig that was so fat you'd think its miniscule stick legs would snap under the strain. I thought it would be the best thing in her collection, the only thing to perhaps gain in value over the years.

Mona apparently hated it. She hated it because it wasn't cute or cuddly, because the pig wasn't sitting down to dinner in a top hat and tails or ice-skating.

'Aye, it's a pig she wants,' he said, and sighed.

'And you're sick of pigs?' I said.

I was feeling smug. I wanted him to hate the pigs and Mona, but I didn't want him to know that.

'She wants – and you're not going to believe this – she wants a Vietnamese pot-bellied pig.'

'Ah,' I said and despite everything I found myself searching my memory for all the china pigs and papier mâché pigs and pig tea towels I might have spied in gift shops and department stores, because I have to admit that lately I had been noticing these items, despite myself.

'I mean,' he said, 'where the hell are we going to put it?'

'Well, I'm sure you could make room for it. How about in the hall?'

I'd been round to their house a month ago when Mona was off on a conference. The hall was the only place that was relatively pig free.

Malcolm had cooked me supper. He'd baked pork chops in the oven with onions and Bramleys. He saw no irony in this. I'd brought a bottle of Chardonnay for us. I'd had to open it using a corkscrew with a pig's grinning head for a handle.

After the supper and the wine, we sat on the sofa together and listened to Portishead's first album. We came this close to kissing. The lights were down low, we both had our feet on the coffee table and he had turned his head towards mine to say something. We were looking into each other's eyes. Each of us searching as if for a signal. He'd moved ever so slightly closer, I'd lifted my chin so that my mouth was aimed more squarely at his. He'd said my name.

'Rachel,' he'd said and it was almost a whisper. He made it sound almost beautiful, or at least like something that signified beauty for him.

But then the phone had rung and it was Mona, of course.

Mona reminding him to put the rubbish out and buy milk for the next day. I heard him say, 'Yeah, I know. I know. I will. I won't forget. Yeah. No. No, of course not. No, I know you don't like it. I wouldn't. Okay now. Okay. Bye.'

No words of love, no 'see you tomorrow', no 'I miss you'.

He replaced the receiver, turned to me and grinned conspiratorially, 'She accused me of cooking meat in her kitchen, with her pans. As if I would!' He smiled, but then he was cleaning up, getting rid of the evidence, putting bones in the rubbish sack, taking the sack out to the pavement, running water in the sink to do the dishes, spraying air freshener around the place.

That sort of thing can put you off someone. You don't want to see a man's fear, a man's dishonesty expressed like that – blown into the air like particles of chemically-enhanced lily of the valley. I made my excuses and left.

The next day I got up early so that I could practise for my grade six music exam.

For a while I'd moved my music stand to the back of the room. I felt ashamed I suppose, because of what Malcolm had said about me showing off. The light wasn't nearly as good there, and the acoustics seemed diminished as if the sounds could only creep out and dared not be bold and beautiful.

I played one testing note, and it came out sounding so hurt and hesitant, that I felt angry enough to pick up the music stand, march across the room and put it back where it belonged, in the window.

I played the same note again and this time it was rich and true and confident.

I played for over an hour. I played with pleasure and without making a single mistake. Everything worked seamlessly as if my fingers had lives of their own. As if the bow was guiding my hand in its dance across the strings instead of vice versa.

I felt as if I could have played forever. Played until my neck and jaw were permanently locked in place on the violin's rest. Played until my fingers bled. I could have done it, I'm certain, but I had to stop to go to work.

I'd set my clock radio to go off when the time was up and its sudden jangle of pop stopped me in my tracks.

I stabbed a finger onto the snooze button, and stood for a moment listening to the silence and breathing deeply as if I was a diver coming up for air.

I glanced out of the window. My flat overlooks the edge of the common. It's not the nicest part, there's only a few trees, and the grass has that scrubby abandoned look to it, like one dog too many had done its business there. But I like that I am close to some expanse of natural land; that I'm not so hemmed in and choked by the city.

I was still holding the violin and the bow, dangling them loosely by my sides. I was contemplating ringing work and telling them I had the flu, but that would mean that someone else would have to sacrifice their day off and it didn't seem fair. Then, as I stared at the common, I noticed a red-haired man walking away in the direction of the town centre. He was too far away for me to see his face, but something about his build; his gait as he strode along, made me think it was Malcolm. But then what would Malcolm be doing there at eight in the morning, when he lived on the other side of town and didn't even have a dog? Unless he wanted to see me; that was possible, but wouldn't he have called? Unless he'd been put off by that vision of me in the window with my snooty girl's violin.

I remembered that now, as we stood in the Prince of Wales and talked about pigs.

'Malcolm,' I said, 'do you ever walk on the common?'

'Huh?'

'It's just that a couple of weeks ago, I thought I saw you.'

Of course, he wasn't really listening to me and maybe I wasn't listening to him, because he had to spell out to me what he meant.

'Look. Are you listening to what I'm saying? She wants a bloody Vietnamese pot-bellied pig. A real one. A pet. She's heard people keep them as pets and now she wants one.'

'Oh,' I said, 'Jesus. That's crazy.'

But he hadn't answered my question. It didn't seem important enough to raise again. Not in the face of the real live pig conversation.

'She's going to see some piglets on a farm just outside Carmarthen. The family is putting her up for the night. I thought maybe later you could come around. Get a take-away maybe and a bottle of wine?'

'I don't know,' I said. I was thinking about unfinished business. If we had kissed that night, we would have done more than kiss. Going the whole way wouldn't have seemed quite so taboo seeing as we'd been lovers before. He had been mine, before he was ever hers.

'I've moved the music stand again,' I said, surprising even myself that I should say it.

'Oh, aye,' he said, 'I know.'

'The light's better there.'

'Uh huh.'

'It makes me happy, you know, to stand there while I play. It's not showing off.'

He looked at me oddly then. He'd obviously forgotten what he'd once said about how I looked when I stood in the window.

'So, do you want to come over later?' he asked and playfully nudged my knee with his.

I thought about all the pigs everywhere. Too many reminders of bloody Mona.

'No,' I said, 'why don't you come around to mine. I can rustle up a curry. I'll play that tune you used to like too.'

This idea made me happy. For him I'd play even more seamlessly than I had the other morning. I'd play the Bach, let the last note hover in the air after I'd lifted the bow from the strings and eased my fingers from their position. Then slowly, I'd put the violin on the table with the bow beside it. I'd walk to him, kneel in front of where he was sitting, touch his neck, offer him my mouth, play him with my body. Lay beside him, like the bow by the violin.

He sighed, then spoke, 'Thing is, Mona will probably ring, so....'

I left the pub just after that. I don't think I really showed him how angry I was, but maybe I was abrupt. Spartan, I suppose you'd call it.

The next time I saw him was four weeks later. I was practising again, this time for my seventh grade. It was dusk. I saw a figure in the distance, walking what I thought was a stubby little dog, a corgi or something like that. When I looked again he was much nearer. He was growing his hair out again. The auburn tint seemed to almost glow in the last of the light. He was coming closer all the time and looking up at the window. When he reached the fence, he stopped and waved.

I waved back. I was about to gesture for him to come up, when he began pointing and nodding to the creature on the end of the leash.

It wasn't a dog at all. Not a corgi or a bull terrier or even a mongrel. No, I should have known it really. What he had on the end of the lead was a funny-looking fat little blackish-brown piglet.

And it clearly had a mind of its own, because the next minute it was jerking and squirming and squealing and tugging. Malcolm struggled for a few seconds to keep it still – to keep himself rooted to the spot beneath my window, but then he gave up, shrugged helplessly, and threw me a quick wave before he let himself be dragged off comically by the absurd and busy little pig.

I heard its squeals as it retreated; high, sharp and discordant. I brought the violin up to my shoulder again, nuzzled my chin in the rest, positioned my fingers high on the neck and scraped the bow across the strings. I made three quick pig squeals, then – show off that I was – I did the Sonata number 2 in A over and over, until the sun set and I could no longer see the park beyond the window, nor any audience, unwanted or otherwise.

Good Enough

This is where they met, in a high glass tower overlooking the new Cardiff Bay development. Him and three other people lined up behind the big ash desk. Him in an expensive suit and pale lilac shirt, smiling and showing his small white teeth, then once, winking at her. She didn't get the job, but he rang her personally to break the news. So kind, so considerate.

'It's out of my hands,' he'd said, 'if I'd had my way...'

'It's okay,' she'd said and would have put the phone down – wanted to put the phone down, but he spoke so quickly, so angrily then.

'No, it's not okay. It's not. You could do that job. You know you could.'

Yes, she thinks, and recognises this truth about herself. She may be lacking in formal qualifications, but she could do so much. This man, she thought, in his smart office with his designer suit and manicured fingernails and his money and his power and his success, he has seen her talent shining through. This touches her. It touches her more than if she'd got the job. Her breath catches in her throat and he says 'listen' and she obeys.

'Listen,' he says again, 'I've got an idea. Mate of mine, see, he's just starting this dot.com. It's going to be big. You can do the business with the old computers, can't you?'

'Well,' she says, and hesitates.

'Yeah,' he says, 'blag it, eh?'

She hesitates, surprised at the slang word, at the inference, 'I've done a bit.'

'There you go,' he says, 'that a girl.'

She smiles into the phone's mouthpiece by way of reply.

'Now, let me see. Best thing would be if we could meet up, yeah? Discuss it over drinks, yeah? What you doing tonight?'

They meet in a pub in Queen street. She wears her interview suit, pins her hair back, and brings her CV in an A4 envelope. She finds him sitting a booth near the back.

'Huh,' he says when he sees her, 'who died?'

'Pardon?' she says.

'You look like you've been to a funeral.'

'Oh,' is all she can find to say.

He looks different. Washed-out grey T-shirt and jeans. He doesn't offer to buy her a drink and so she asks him if he'd like one.

'Yeah,' he says, 'Becks.'

He takes it without thanking her. Tips the bottle up, glugs.

'So,' he says, 'how old are you?'

'Twenty-three.'

'Where you from?'

'Cardiff,' she says.

'Doh! I know that, what part?'

'Oh, Roath,' she says.

'Tiger Bay boy, I am,' he says, 'and baby, look at me now.' She smiles, uncomprehendingly. 'You see what you want and you've got to grab it. You've got to fight. No one's gonna give it you on a plate, like.' She nods and wonders whether she should raise the issue of the job. 'I'm hungry,' he says, 'let's go eat.'

She gathers up her jacket and bag and envelope and follows him out of the pub. They walk towards the castle, and all the time he's talking.

'So that's what you learn in karate. Like that you can kill but you choose not to, yeah? Same with business. Sometimes it's softly, softly, catchee monkey, other times it's...,' and here he draws a finger across his throat with relish.

He steps into an Indian restaurant with vibrant pink flamingo walls and huge dripping abstract canvases.

She feels as if she is being drawn down a strange road against her will. She ate before she came out and has very little money. She does have a credit card, but shouldn't use it, except that, perhaps this is an investment, and besides, he'll pay, won't he?

He orders a starter with king prawns, poppadoms, the relish tray, lager, wine, a speciality main course – the most expensive on the menu. She asks for chicken korma, boiled rice, tap water.

'You girls, eh,' he says, 'eating like a little sparrow. Watching your weight, huh?'

After they have eaten and the dishes are cleared, he lays his hand in the middle of the table palm up, and looks in her eyes.

Finally, she thinks, and puts the A4 envelope on his waiting hand. There is a moment of confusion.

'What's this?' he says.

'My CV.'

He tosses it to one side. 'I wanted to hold your hand.'

'Oh,' she says, and meekly she places her hand, palm to palm, on his.

'Bluest eyes I ever saw,' he said.

'They're green,' she says.

'No, they're not.'

'Yes, they are.'

'They look blue to me.'

'Maybe it's the light,' she concedes.

'I think I'm in love,' he says.

She imagines that he is talking about some other aspect of his life, that he is sharing with her the story of his love for some other woman.

'Oh,' she says, because she expects him to say more.

'Is that all you can say?' he says and he squeezes her hand.

He pays for the meal, but spoils it by bragging about how he's putting it on the company's credit card.

When they leave and begin to walk down Mary Street, he throws an arm around her shoulder so that her neck is caught in the bend of his arm. His hand hangs loosely down, cupping the air in front of her breast.

She is growing a little impatient with the situation. Her bus goes in half an hour and no mention has been made of the friend, the dot.com, and the possible job.

'So,' she says, 'what about this mate of yours and the job?'

He stops abruptly, slaps his hand theatrically against his brow.

'Damn,' he says, 'I meant to bring the... ah, thingy. Listen, come back to mine and I can give you the stuff then.'

Come into my parlour said the spider to the fly, is what she thinks when he says this.

He is a handsome spider. Tall, a lean body, dark hair cropped short, a moustache and goatee beard, clean smelling. He talks a lot, smiles a lot, but his smile reminds her of Jim Carey. There is something clownish and pasted-on about it. She pushes this thought to the back of her mind. Swallows her mean and distrustful thoughts, just as she swallowed the dinner when she wasn't hungry.

'Okay,' she says.

'That a girl,' he says and squeezes her neck.

They get a cab to Emerald Street. The house is not how she imagined. What furniture there is, is mismatched, worn and shabby, but he tells her in endless detail about the work he will have done, the furniture he will buy; this wall knocked down, the floors refinished, a black leather and chrome settee from Habitat, wooden blinds.

He pours her a vodka, duty free. Says he's thinking of getting a place in New York. Knows someone who knows someone who will get him a job and a green card.

Time slips away like chilled vodka down a throat. He makes a move, she lets him.

In the morning he forgets to mention the job, but says he'll ring her.

Two weeks go by before he rings.

'Hey,' he says.

'I thought you'd forgotten.'

'Me? Forget you? You're kidding. Listen, my mate, yeah? He's out of the country, yeah? He's got some business contacts in South Africa, yeah? But I spoke to him and he will be hiring and he wants some more details, yeah. So how 'bout we get together again?'

This time they meet in the pub near his house. One drink, and he says, let's go back to mine. This time she hasn't eaten because she assumed he'd want to eat out again. None of his new furniture has arrived yet, the place looks even worse than before. He gets some vodka from the freezer, it's Tesco's own brand, the cheapest, with a plain white label and the word vodka in black type.

He makes a move, she lets him.

'Mmm,' he says, 'I missed you.'

He tells her there's a do coming up. Asks her if she's got anything good to wear. Designer stuff, he says, dress to impress.

The next day she buys a new dress. Forty-five quid reduced from three hundred. She hangs it in the wardrobe with the tags still on. He doesn't ring for a month.

'Baby,' he says, 'I've been missing you.' He asks her to drop around his at one o'clock that afternoon. 'I've got a surprise for you,' he promises.

The surprise turns out to be a leather and chrome settee. The rest of the room is the same old tat, sticky grey carpet, and battered armchair, stained coffee table. He's also got a brand new camera. He persuades her to lie naked on the settee while he takes photos of her. She lets him, but draws the line at opening her legs.

'But I love you,' he says. In one hand he holds the camera and with the other he tries to push her knees apart.

'No,' she says.

'Ah, come on,' he pleads.

'No, I don't want to.'

'Don't you trust me, baby?'

'Yes, but I don't want to do that.'

She gets a job in the multiplex cinema. Minimum wage, but with the promise of an increase with each 'Oscar' you win by passing training tests.

He doesn't ring for two months. She thinks about the photos he took. Sometimes she wants to see them because she imagines he made her look beautiful. Other times she remembers the harshness of the flash, her skin marked by the tight elastic of her shed underwear.

On the phone she affects coldness, but he does not seem to notice. It's a Sunday afternoon; he's ringing from a pub. In the background she can hear a roar of voices and music playing.

'Come on,' he says, 'come to the pub. Come on, you sweet thing.' His voice is liquid, sloshing about in her sober ears.

'Okay,' she says and she feels free suddenly, able to take command.

'Atta girl,' he says and she says, 'Atta boy,' and means to lace the phrase with sarcasm, but he's too far gone to notice.

The pub is small, too far from the city centre to have undergone the indignity of improvement. There are no big screen TVs or sofas or chrome stools, just the old ripped banquettes, round Formica-topped tables, Brain's ashtrays, a dart board, a pool table, and a juke box with a lot of Johnny Cash and Tom Jones and Elvis amongst its selection.

He is leaning against the bar and when she joins him, he roars with drunken appreciation and catches her neck in the crook of his arm and gives her a squeeze.

'Whey!' he yells, 'Atta girl!' Then he calls the barmaid, 'Eh, eh, Patsy.'

Patsy, who is pulling a pint for another customer, slides her eyes towards him with malice. She's in her fifties, with stiff yellowing hair in tight curls. She's wearing blue jeans that strain against a full round belly and a red cowboy shirt with embroidery over her hard-looking breasts. Around her neck she has tied a white chiffon scarf. The barman is wearing a black felt cowboy hat and a button-down gingham shirt with silver studs.

'Eh, Patsy!'

He slaps a hand against the counter, 'a drink for my bird when you're ready.'

The woman's mouth tightens, turning it into a fleshless straight line. She finishes with the customer she was serving, puts the money in the till, picks up a cloth and comes to him. She wipes the bar and makes a barely perceptible flick of the head towards him.

'Pint of Stella, and...' he says, 'what you want?'

'Coke.'

'And a vodka and coke.'

She sips her drink, and, despite the noise, despite the music and the laughter and his arm around her shoulder, she feels as lonely as she has ever done. There is wall of mirrors behind the bar and she catches sight of herself, small and pale and smeared, while all around there is colour and movement. Then as she watches, she sees that while he's still got his arm around her, he's leaning back on his stool and pointing at her to someone on the other side of the bar. Pointing and grinning and nodding his head emphatically. His gesture is saying – this is the one. And she imagines him with those photos of her. She sees the pictures being passed from hand to hand; fingered, smirked over, leered at, laughed at.

She wriggles around on the stool and turns to face him, to catch him in the act, but he's tipping his head back, downing a beer and when he's done, he slams his glass on the bar and wipes a hand across the back of his loose mouth.

He orders more drinks. This time he gets her a double vodka and she drinks it fast, and when he's in the gents' she orders another. Doesn't buy him one. Patsy grins at her conspiratorially, and touches her hand when she gives her the change.

There is a moment's silence then, as the record on the jukebox changes and people's voices drop to murmurs.

This is the quiet before the storm, the eye of the hurricane, because the next record to come on causes an explosion of recognition. It's 'Delilah' by the beloved native son, Tom Jones.

Amongst the noise of the singing, he comes back and hoists himself giddily onto his stool. Says something she does not hear and squeezes her thigh in what is meant to be a friendly gesture, but will leave a thumb and four-fingered bruise.

She is the only person not singing along as the verses progress. But then she is caught up in the plaintive words of the chorus, the echoed drunken roar of the old soaks and the young soaks.

Why, why, why? Delilah! My, my, my Delilah!

They even add words to the musical parts, yelling out 'diddle liddle liddle liddle liddle', then back to the refrain 'my, my, my Delilah'.

Next on the jukebox it's Johnny Cash and June Carter doing 'Jackson', and now there are three couples up and dancing, wriggling their middle-aged bodies in a space between the bar and the pool table.

All of the people in the pub are mouthing the song's words 'we got married in a fever'.

She is enjoying the spectacle and thinks that if she got drunk enough and could stay drunk forever, then she too would roar and jig and smile and stumble against a chair and slosh beer onto her clothes and not care.

Then 'The green, green grass of home' comes on and the mood becomes more sombre. This is the wake for lost souls, the pity and the love for the idyllic homeland, the drunk's descent into bathos.

He puts a hand on the back of her neck as though she were a stray kitten and pulls her to him and breathes into her ear, 'Come on baby, let's go back to mine.'

He staggers a little when they're back on the street, but recovers. It's bright outside, there's a dazzling tinder dry sunlight that bounces off bruised cars and cracked pavements.

His home looks even more vagrant than before. On the coffee table there's a carton of milk gone sour and a Domino's box lying agape with a half-eaten pizza cold and greasy in its maw.

The cushions on the leather settee have slipped out of place and on one end there's a pillow with a night-time silhouette of a city skyline on it, New York probably.

'I's mad that pub,' he says ''s'laugh though init?'

He stands swaying slightly over the coffee table, then swoops down and picks up a limp triangle of pizza and gorges on it.

'Eh,' he says, 'I shouldn't drink really. No' ona Sunday lunchtime. S'bloody lethal, that bloody pub. D'you wanna coffee or somefing?'

'You got any vodka?' she says brightly.

'Ah, there's a girl eh? Eh?' He reels off towards the kitchen, and she hears doors opened too violently, a fridge rattling in protest at being slammed shut.

She notices his camera on top of the gas fire next to an ashtray and thinks about smashing it to pieces. Then he's back with a bottle of vodka, and one wineglass and a Cardiff FC mug. He sloshes vodka into both, hands her the glass and sits heavily beside her.

'D'you wanna watch a video or something?' he says waving a hand vaguely at the TV and the piles of videos heaped around and on top of it.

'Yeah, okay,' she says, 'can I pick one?'

She kneels by the TV and sorts through his collection: *Terminator. Evil Dead. Star Wars. Star Trek. A Fistful of Dollars. ET.* She chooses *Jaws* and puts it on and presses rewind. She listens to the whirr and clunk of the mechanism and stares at her reflection in the black screen. Behind her she can see his slumped figure slowly collapsing into the prized sofa, the vodka-filled mug resting on one thigh with a hand loosely around its handle.

She presses play and the film starts. His breathing grows noisier and more drawn out.

'Hey,' she says, then when he shows no response, she adds, 'Atta boy.'

She begins a thorough investigation of his house. The kitchen sink is piled high with greasy dishes and seems to be blocked, as it's half-full of opaque water. On the surface there is a regatta of tea bags and pale, disintegrating chips. A kitchen drawer holds bills. It is stuffed to the gills with bills and a lot of them are red.

She slips upstairs and opens a wardrobe door to an avalanche of spilled clothes. The bed is a wreck; the duvet is covered with the same Manhattan skyline print as the pillow downstairs and is bunched up in a heap, and the sheet, a lurid purple swirl, is exposed showing a yard-long rip.

There's a bedside cabinet and the top drawer holds those intimate clues to the life of a bachelor. Condoms in a range of colours, flavours and styles. Lubricant. Used tissues. Vitamin pills. A sachet of lemon-flavoured hangover cure, which has ripped open and spilled its yellow crystals. Some batteries. A postcard from Thailand signed by someone called 'Suz'.

The next drawer is empty except for an open plastic packet of boxer shorts with one pair missing. He's taken to buying new pants rather than washing the ones he's got, she thinks.

The third drawer is half-filled with socks, but all of them are odd. She fishes her hand in, stirring the socks and beneath them she finds what she's been looking for and sits on the edge of the bed to inspect it properly.

It's a brightly-printed wallet with the words 'Your memories' on it a candy coloured text. There's a picture of a small child holding a bright red balloon against a sky that is too blue.

She opens it and looks at the photos inside. There's two photos of the new Millennium Stadium and another of a game in progress; it's nothing but a blur of green with figures like specks and the back of someone's head too close and bleached out by the flash.

Then there's a picture that she took of him, which she had quite forgotten.

He'd wanted one of himself on his new settee and he'd sat with one arm along its back denoting ownership, doing a dazzling grin for the camera. Behind his head an old Southern Comfort mirror hung at a tipsy angle, ruining the classy look he was going for.

Next there was a photo of her and it was the first he'd taken, and she was still dressed and had covered her face with hands.

The final print showed one of his feet and the edge of the coffee table and the grey carpet.

Only six photos. Six photos, but there must be more.

Downstairs, the *Jaws* theme music rises to a crescendo and she pictures the shark's fin breaking the surface of the water, swerving and circling, and shudders at the thought.

In the front of the photo envelope there's a second shallow sleeve and here she finds the negatives. Now her heart is thumping and she holds the plastic sleeve up to the light; the first strip has images on it, the ones she has already seen. But the rest are clear; a pale orange emptiness free of memory and sin. She replaces it in the drawer and goes downstairs again.

He has slid further down the couch and the mug has tipped and there's a dark wet stain on his thigh and crutch.

She surveyed him with a cold eye, and then she picked up the camera, checked it for film, turned the flash on and waited for the green light to appear. She took some time to compose her picture carefully, crouching down at the same level as his crutch so that she could get the full effect of the stain and his face collapsed in drunken sleep above. She took three shots to be certain she'd got it just right.

'Atta boy,' she says and she drinks the last inch of vodka from the wineglass.

Outside the sun is still blazing down and she has nothing to remember or regret, just the good yellow light of a fading afternoon, which is all she ever wants or needs. It's not great, but good enough. For now.

A Slow Dance

During the Christmas of 1965 when I was eleven a girl called Sandra befriended me. I don't know why she had made me her friend just then, maybe it was because her other friends had gone away for the holidays and I was the only one who was lonely enough and malleable enough to be picked up, only to be put down again once school started.

I had been invited for a sleepover on Boxing Day as Sandra's family were having a bit of a do and it was thought that she would enjoy it more if she had a little friend to keep her company. Looking back I seem to remember that even as my mother gushed with excitement at this invite to the other side of the tracks, I was feeling a sort of preternatural unease. It was as if I recognized that the old me was somehow about to slip away, and this new girl; prettier, brighter, with newer, shinier clothes would soon step into the limelight. But at that age, one can't quite state it, or even understand it in such eloquent terms, so it is instead a mere shadow, a shifting of the light, or an unfamiliar smell in the air, the smoky scent of wet summer pavements for example, or the taste of a first olive.

Sandra's uncle had collected me at six, and after the relative quiet of their house on my arrival, by eight the place seemed to be throbbing and rocking with people, and the radiogram in the best room was playing Matt Monroe. I had never seen anything like it before in my life.

Many of the women wore furs and smelled of sweet powdery perfume and hairspray and blew lipstick-tinged smoke into the air. All of the men were bow tied and whiskered and red faced, it seemed. And everyone was loud and grew louder as the evening progressed.

Sandra and I were given the job of answering the door each time the bell rang. Then when the guests shed their coats, we took them up to Sandra's parent's room and laid them in a great heap on the big double bed. We buried our faces in the furs, breathing in the greasy animal smell that deep down was little diluted by either perfume or death.

Then the doorbell would ring and we'd go helter-skelter down the stairs to open it and my arms would be filled with more furs and tweeds and cashmeres, and hers with brightly wrapped gifts. For a while we lolled about the on the mountain of coats dreaming of how our future lives would be.

The noise from downstairs increased; the music grew louder, and the men's laughs – haw, haw – rumbled up through the floorboards, while the women's higher pitched giggles shot through all the other sounds like sharp arrows. Faintly heard and underscoring the other sounds were rhythmic thumps and thuds and heavy footfalls.

Sandra said, 'They're dancing now,' and she looked long-suffering; like a young mother worn to shreds of exhaustion by an irrepressible toddler.

'Yeah,' I said and nodded gravely, but I was thinking about how no one ever danced in my house. Not unless my parents did it solemnly, secretly, humming under their breath, shuffling their feet in tartan slippers over the hearth rug in a furtive waltz.

'Hey!' I said, faking sudden inspiration, 'Let's go down and see them.'

Sandra thought about this and as she did so she picked up the mink stole and put it around her shoulders, then rubbed her chin back and forth seductively over the deep soft fur. She sighed, 'Only if you really want to.'

How could I answer that? Her words gave the impression that she might bend to my will, but she also managed to impart a suggestion that she would do this only under sufferance, and that I would owe her for it and what the hell sort of freak was I anyway for wanting it?

'Well, I'm bored up here,' I said, flinging the sleeve of an ocelot from my lap where I'd been cradling it.

She poked her tongue out at me, but I took that as a good omen, a sign that I'd won.

'Come on, then,' she said.

The noise grew louder. When we opened the bedroom door the volume seemed to be cranked up a few turns.

Then as we descended the stairs it was as if we were walking towards a loudspeaker and when we finally opened the door to the living room it was like we were entering the loudspeaker itself. We were inside the music and the voices and the thud, thud of dancing feet.

For me it was like entering Hell. Not in the religious sense or the tormented sense, but it reminded me of pictures I'd seen of Hell with the great press of bodies writhing in an assortment of attitudes, and the smoke and the shouts added to that impression. Here of course everybody was having a fine old time and when we stood momentarily still at the threshold we could feel the floorboards jumping and straining beneath our feet.

Sandra's mother spotted us and pushed through the dancers to greet us. She was effervescent with drink and threw her arms around Sandra and clung to her as if they had just been reunited after years of absence and torment.

'Oh, my darling girl!' she shouted and Sandra grinned sheepishly.

Her mother's dress reminded me of a fish, it was covered all over with tiny silver sequins like scales and clung to her body like a second skin. I was a little shocked to see that the dress had no back to it, which meant she was wearing neither a bra nor a corset or a petticoat or a vest, garments which my mother had led me to believe were as necessary to life as air to breathe or water to drink. The skin of her back was smooth and tanned and sleek with a faint sheen of sweat.

When her mother released Sandra she turned to me as though suddenly deciding that I was also a little prodigal daughter returned from the desert, and threw her arms around me.

'Oh, my other darling girl,' she said, 'are you having a super time?' I couldn't answer or barely breathe as she had my face pressed firmly against her bosom. She was wearing a spiky silver brooch that was meant to represent either a star or flower and this would have taken my eye out if it had met my face just one inch lower. As it was it left a red fan-shaped impression of itself on my forehead that I noticed a little later when I saw myself in the mirror over the fireplace. Finally she let me go.

'Are you girls going to have a little drinky?' she offered, then answered her own question by flitting off on wobbly stilettos to get us one. When she came back she had two champagne glasses filled with a pale yellow fizzy drink. I thought it was some sort of special lemonade and that she'd given it to us in those glasses to make us feel grown up.

As soon as my nose got near the top of the glass it was pinged by little explosions of fizz and it smelled nothing like lemonade, but heavy and shuddery and dark like communion wine.

I looked at Sandra and she did a vampish pout and fluttered her eyelashes. I did the same. Then Sandra pinched her nose as if she was about to jump in at the deep end of the pool, and she tipped the glass to her lips and took two big gulps.

I copied, pinching my nose and trying to swallow the stuff, but I ended up spluttering and coughing and one of the uncles came and whacked me on the back, which did not help.

But then I managed to drink the Babycham and Sandra drank some more and after a while we did the Hokey-Kokey and the Conga and the Twist and the room seemed different. I was now part of the noise and laughter and none of it seemed frightening or strange anymore.

Then a slower song came on. It had a big explosive opening of trumpets and trombones and the man was singing about how he was poor. He was saying something about going from rags to riches and being a beggar. Then they played Kathy Kirby's 'Secret Love' and a few people joined in, roaring like a football crowd and flinging their arms about.

Now I'll shout it from the highest hills, even tell the golden daffodils.

I always understood these songs in their most literal way and that often confused me. When the Kathy Kirby record was playing Sandra's mother went and stood next to the radiogram and put her hand over her heart like she had indigestion.

I wanted them to play the Chubby Checker record again. Or the one about how the singer wanted to be Bobby's girl. Or the Alma Cogan, but it was all slow, sad songs from then on. Frank Sinatra, Andy Williams, Tony Bennett and that one about the girl from Ipanenaa, which always made me want to be that girl, even though I knew I never could be.

Sandra sneaked us two more glasses of Babycham. My head was spinning and when I watched the couples in the middle of the room holding onto each and rocking I felt seasick.

Sandra and I went and sat in the bay window behind the long curtain. I think it was Sandra's idea that we would hide and the grownups would search and search for us and we'd peep through the curtains watching them. We sat there for a long time but no one noticed we'd gone.

Then Sandra fell asleep. She'd been sucking her thumb and stroking the tip of her nose with her forefinger. Her eyelids kept lowering in slow blinks and her head was lolling.

'Don't go to sleep,' I said.

''M'not,' she said in a grumpy voice, slurred with tiredness.

I sat there for a while watching her body slide gently down the wall, and then I curled up in a little ball with my head on the bristly carpet. I closed my eyes and tried to fall asleep, but nothing happened. There was less noise from the room now, not so much talking and laughing and the volume on the record player had been turned down a little.

I crawled out from behind the curtain. The room was both emptier and darker than before. The big overhead light – a fancy gilt and crystal chandelier – had been turned off, but the fairy lights and the Christmas tree with its multicoloured bulbs were still switched on. The effect was like a magical cave lit with starlight and glow-worms.

Sandra's mother was dancing in the centre of the room with a man I hadn't noticed before. She had her arms thrown around his neck and his were on her bare back. I could see that he was really feeling her skin, moving his

231

hands in slow exploratory strokes. This shocked me. I had never seen, in the flesh, a man touching a woman this way. I sensed there was something wrong about it, but didn't really know what, and so I just stood there watching. Her eyes were closed and she was hanging off his neck, her feet barely moving. It was the man who was rocking to the music; the woman might have been, like Sandra, fast asleep.

I didn't notice Sandra's father until he was standing in front of me, blocking my view of her mother in the shimmering fish dress.

'Well, young lady, how about a dance?' he asked, grinning down at me.

His smile was a sloppy elastic one, his eyes not quite focused, not really seeing me. Before I could answer him he had scooped me up with one arm hooked under my legs while the other pressed my body to his. My feet dangled uselessly and I had no choice but to put my arms around his shoulders and hang on. He swayed to and fro and while he moved he half hummed, half whispered the words of the song. He smelled of whisky and Lux soap and the bristles on his chin scratched my face. I felt helpless and mute. This was how things were between men and women, I thought; if a man chose you, if they wanted to dance with you then you just had to submit.

He turned me around and around and as we revolved I'd catch glimpses of Sandra's mother. Sometimes the strange man had his hands on her neck, sometimes on her sides just below her armpits and then at the lowest point of her dress where you could almost see her bottom.

The whole time Sandra's father continued to croon along with the song. I could feel his voice resonate in his chest and his breath hot on my ear and neck. I felt silly more than anything, though as long as Sandra saw none of it I didn't mind so much.

We turned again and I saw that the strange man was kissing Sandra's mother on the neck and his fingers were wriggling and struggling to probe beneath the edge of her dress.

Suddenly I wanted to be free. I felt frightened in the same way I felt when I'd strayed into the deep end of the swimming pool and could no longer feel the tiled floor beneath my toes.

We turned yet again so that now I was facing the curtained window where Sandra was hidden. Her father, I thought, will see now. He'll see that another man is kissing his wife and he'll get cross. He'll be like a man in a film. He'll have to fight the other man. Maybe he'll draw a gun and shoot him dead.

The song stopped and another began this one even sadder and slower than before. He'd stopped turning me around and around, and was swaying gently from side to side. He couldn't have known the words to this song because he was humming in a lost way, and it sounded like an insect buzzing, lightly and delicately in my ear. Then he stopped humming and I felt something warm and wet on my neck and it reminded me of a spaniel puppy that had once licked my face and I realized that Sandra's father was kissing me and licking me just like that puppy.

Then I knew I wasn't just out of my depth, I was

drowning. Sinking fast with pinioned arms and some slimy sea creature, an octopus or giant eel suckered to my neck. So instead of being calm like a grown up woman, instead of letting myself be submerged beneath the darkness and the music and the mollusk mouth on my skin, I did what a little girl does when she can no longer feel the bottom of the pool. I kicked, I thrashed and wriggled and screamed.

He dropped me suddenly, and so – landing off balance and still waving my arms in panic – I went reeling backwards in one of those can't-stop-yourself comic stumbling quick steps. It must have looked like I'd danced quite purposely into the elegant silver Christmas tree. It came crashing down on top of me, its stick arms and tinsel-wrapped wire branches pinning me neatly to the carpet.

Sandra's father said, 'What the hell?'

Her mother broke away from the strange man who loped off in the direction of the kitchen. Then Sandra crawled out from under the curtain, looking bleary eyed with sleep.

There was a moment when no one moved. The record stopped. There was a curious silence as though an alien soundlessness had iced over time, locked us in a beat between one note and another. Around me the Christmas tree lights continued to pulse; off and on, off and on.

Then Sandra's father came to untangle me from the tree and her mother followed to help him. Finally, smirking slightly, Sandra joined them and I was free.

A child cannot explain a grown man's lips on the skin of her neck. It is unfathomable to an eleven-year-old. A mistake amongst the rough and tumble of the beer and Babycham, and the blind night and the love songs. It is only with the hindsight of ten years growing that the shameful horror reveals itself. Yet I do not think the man had been kissing me precisely or particularly.

I remember myself and the Christmas tree both on our feet again; the tree a little warped, its top-most branch curving down, the tinsel star half hanging off, and me; a little scratched, a little bruised, the ribbon in my hair drooping over my eyes. And then Sandra and her mother and father had all started to laugh, and I laughed too.

Everything that had happened in the seconds before falling had been wiped away. I might have forgotten it too, but as I stood there laughing, but somewhat mortified, my hand went to my neck in a habitual, nervous and self-protective gesture and my fingers found a wet spot; the memory of a kiss upon my skin like the silver track of a snail after the creature has long gone.

Gestation

Five words an hour, forty words a day, two hundred and eighty a week, fourteen or fifteen thousand words in a year. Translate that into pages in a book. It isn't much. And to be frank, it just doesn't add up. *Madame Bovary*, in the newly translated paperback edition is two hundred and ninety-six pages.

I've done the maths, though admittedly maths is not my strong point. Two hundred and ninety-six pages at an average of three hundred and eighty words a page is over a hundred and ten thousand words. The maths say that Flaubert took seven and a half years to write *Madame Bovary*.

Other accounts claim that the book was written in just five years between 1851 and 1856. Well, perhaps Flaubert worked longer days than I have estimated. Or perhaps, and here is the point where my husband and I tend to squabble, perhaps Flaubert wrote *more* than five words an hour.

To further pursue the subject of mathematics my husband is re-reading *Madame Bovary* for the sixteenth summer in a row. And for the sixteenth summer in a row we are holidaying in Wales.

It's the mountains we come for. And the memories.

My memories only stretch back over sixteen years. His reach further. Sometimes I imagine his memories like long arms; unnaturally long arms that are elastic and can delve into places that for me are beyond reach.

He reaches into his jar of memories and sometimes he'll produce a fragment for me and offer it to me like some saint's relic.

For a few years he would only hint, in a pained and reticent way, about a guilty secret – something so terrible, and that so shamed him as to make its telling beyond the pale. 'I have done a thing...' he would begin, and then he would let his face fall into his hands as if he could not bear for me to see it. 'Darling,' I would say, but such endearments only made it worse, and he would groan, and utter curses against himself, calling himself a despicable man, a beast, an animal. Sometimes I wondered if he had murdered someone. The only thing I knew for sure was that this terrible thing which he had done had happened in Wales.

After while, whenever he said things like that I found myself struck dumb. Then I began to hear voices forming in my head that wanted to say mean things.

'So what?' I wanted to say, 'who cares?'

I don't know why it made me so angry; maybe because I felt duped by him. Still feel duped. There is nothing more frustrating than being set up to hear an intimacy, a terrible and painful intimacy, only to have it snatched away before the dénouement.

I had first met him at a Christmas party. I was twenty-two and my boyfriend at the time didn't understand why I had to spend so much time reading, studying, writing essays, but it was my third year and the exams were looming up ahead. So I suppose I was looking for someone who would take me seriously. Or so I thought then.

Cause and effect. You can't escape it even if you are aware of it.

If my boyfriend at the time hadn't been so hell bent on having a good time; going to the pub, to parties, clubs, the cinema, hanging out with his mates, then perhaps an older man, wouldn't have held quite so much appeal.

Of course love and lust and desire aren't supposed to work like that. It's meant to be the body, the face, the voice – all those physical attributes that set things off – the gaze in particular; the eyes that make their own language, their own trouble.

So there we were – the professor and I – at this Christmas party, talking about books. I was doing a degree in education, so while I read a great deal of novels, they weren't literature *per se*. I'd just finished *Sophie's Choice* which I discovered he hadn't read. I suppose I must have been gushing, but I couldn't believe that an expert in literature hadn't read this book, and I wanted to persuade him against what I perceived as his loss and his folly. I overlooked, I suppose, his greater wisdom. I did not understand that certain professors of literature do not bother themselves with contemporary novels, but are so absorbed in the nineteenth, or the seventeenth, or fourteenth centuries that they can barely stir themselves to acknowledge the world around them. (He would argue of course that these classics say everything that needs to be said about the human condition, and that there are, according to some theorists, only a handful of stories which are told and retold anyway.) I imagined my words were finding their target; that I was David with my little verbal slingshot, and my Goliath was going to succumb.

He mentioned Flaubert, Othello, Lear, Kafka. Those are the names I remember. I hadn't read any of it, but I wasn't stupid, I had notions of where they all fit, but I probably pretended more knowledge than I really had. Nodded a great deal. Widened my eyes, said, 'ah yes, mm, Kafka. Exactly.'

And I was clever enough to shut up when I got totally lost.

I remember him saying how every young woman should read Bovary. That was how he put it. Exactly.

The next day I went to the library and in the author index catalogue I looked up Bovary. It still makes me cringe with embarrassment to remember it. I even went to the counter and asked the librarian where the books by Bovary would be. The librarian, a middle-aged man with those strange half-spectacles, grey hair, a red bulbous nose, was very kind, very polite.

'I think what you might be looking for,' he said, 'is a book called *Madame Bovary*. By Flaubert.'

He led me to the correct section, ran his finger along the spines of the books, first from left to right, then back again.

'Oh dear,' he said, 'no luck this time. It's out on loan. But we can reserve it for you.'

'That's okay,' I said, an idea was forming in my head. 'I have a friend. I'm sure he'll lend me a copy.'

And that was it, I stepped onto a different path, changed direction, came to here; this moment, this particular life instead of a different one.

Looking back I am shocked by how bold I was, how undaunted by convention.

I went to the college, found his department, the stairs leading up, the corridor which was long, narrow, lit only by fluorescent strips, with doors leading off at regular intervals, all of them with names on them. It was very quiet, hardly a soul about, must have been before the students came back. It was only by chance that he was there at all that day; the heating system in his flat had packed up and he'd left the workmen to it. Couldn't stand the noise. And it was cold.

I knocked on the door, didn't hesitate, didn't give a damn.

A voice inside the room called out for me to come in, which I did.

He didn't recognize me at first. Didn't remember me. But despite that I could tell he was pleased to see me – happy to invite a young attractive woman into his monk's cell.

You might think it's rather arrogant of me to describe myself as 'young and attractive'. I wouldn't have said it at the time, but sixteen years gives one a perspective, doesn't it? Besides which he was a man in his forties, and not exactly a handsome man at that; though he had grown into his face somewhat and he had a good head of hair and nice eyes.

He had five copies of the Flaubert. Five! That shocked me. Two of them were in the original French. One was very fancy, it had been issued by a small publisher and had pictures in it, woodcuts or lithographs by some famous artist I hadn't heard of, though I didn't show that of course. Another version he had was a paperback and the pages had yellowed, and the cover was stained and torn, and it was filled with narrow strips of paper marking particular passages, and the margins and seemingly every bit of unprinted paper was covered with scribbled notes.

That had shocked me as I had been raised to think that only stupid people damaged books, vandalised them in that way!

Here's what he once told me, 'a book is only alive when it's being read.'

He lent me the third translated version. There was a girl's name written inside the front cover. She'd put her name, and the date, and her hall of residence. She had the sort of handwriting I always associate with grammar school girls. It was neat, a little too large, and very regular, all of the 'o's' and 'a's' had broad open faces, all the 't's' were straight and tall. She would be the sort of woman who would carefully fold her clothes and place them on a chair before sex.

'You can keep it,' he'd said, as I stood there lingering, opening and closing the book and trying to think of something to say.

Of course I didn't want to keep the book. Giving it back would be my excuse to see him again.

'Oh, thanks,' I said, but I must have sounded disappointed, sarcastic even.

'She won't be back,' he said.

I must have frowned, shown my confusion.

'Who?'

'The student – I've had that copy a few years now. She must have left. I can't even remember her name.'

I opened the book when he said that; read the name aloud, 'Lucy Clark.'

He made a face when I said the name, to show he didn't remember her and didn't care either.

Perhaps it was that that made me say what I said next.

'Maybe I want to give it back,' I said. He blushed and I felt immediately that I had gone too far, and started backpedaling. 'I mean,' I said, 'that I may have questions, and would appreciate your greater knowledge.'

'Well, I am fl-fl-flattered,' he said with difficulty, but without embarrassment.

So he had a stammer. One that he had mastered almost completely but still it raised its awkward little head, now and then. I found it endearing. Fell in love with him at that very moment.

'Did you manage to get the book I mentioned?' I asked, and as soon as the words left my mouth I was struck by how I suddenly sounded like the erudite professor handing out book recommendations, assignments.

'Ahm... the book?' he asked.

'We talked about it at the party,' I said.

'Oh yes, of course, but you'll have to forgive me, the title seems to have slipped my mind.'

'*Sophie's Choice*,' I said. He looked unenthused, but I was on a roll, undeterred. 'I'll write it down,' I said and began to scramble through my bag in order to find a pen, though all I kept grabbing at blindly were lipsticks and tampons.

'That's okay,' he said, and I saw that he was sitting, pen raised, paper poised waiting for me to say it again.

'*Sophie's Choice*,' I said, 'by William Styron.'

'There,' he said, 'thank you,' and he slid the piece of paper to the back of his desk.

Of course, he never did get the book, never read it, which is a pity. But even more tellingly, I should confess now, that despite everything it was a very long time before I got around to reading *Madame Bovary*.

At first my not reading it was to do with me putting it off so that I could do the book justice. I had some future vision of myself in which I was transformed into some heavyweight intellectual; elegant, straight-backed, sitting in a chintz armchair with the book raised to eye level and stillness and silence all around, only broken by the sounds of pages turning, the clock ticking, my own steady breathing.

For a time I felt guilty about my failure to read it, then I began to resent the guilt, and very quickly that turned into anger, and now it's calcified into a sort of enduring stubbornness. Now it is a matter of principle.

And that sense of principle; that separateness that stands like a wall between us, was begun by him, even if it was and is kept alive by me.

It was he who suggested Wales for our first holiday together. I'd wanted to go to Greece, or more precisely Crete as I was reading Mary Renault's novels then and wanted to see Knossos; breathe its ancient air, and I'll freely admit, get a sun tan while I was at it.

Of course, being in love and being utterly in awe of the man, when he said mildly, casually that he'd rather imagined himself in the Welsh hills that summer, I very quickly adjusted my own visions; away went the golden feet in flat leather sandals, the sea as warm as my own private tub, delectable fish and squid eaten in some harbour side restaurant, and the painted temples and palaces; deserted, dramatic; myself drenched in history, bare breasted, bull jumping and snake charming.

Well, you'll have to forgive me, I was young, and I'm trying to be honest.

Did I ask him why he wanted to go to Wales? Probably not.

Did he offer me any more information about the terrible sin he had committed there? Definitely not. And it seems to me that there is more than just carelessness in that; that there is something deliberate and calculated about his failure to mention it.

He would argue with that, of course. He would draw himself up to his full height, stretch his neck, peer at me over the top of his glasses; blink, as if to check that this angry little creature, this pipsqueak virago was really and truly his wife. And true to form, I'd get louder, more and more frustrated with him.

'But I just don't understand *why* you bring it up, then refuse to share it with me. I am your wife for goodness sake!'

And the more angry; the more insistent and unreasonable I became, the calmer he would be.

'Damn you,' I'd say then, carefully editing the words I'd really wanted to say which were 'fuck you'. What I'd have liked to say is 'fuck you and your dark secrets routine' but that would be going too far; would reveal more about me and my true self than I would wish him to see. Even now.

Sometimes I convince myself that his bloody precious Emma Bovary would use bad language; that she would be flawed like me, would swear like a bloody fishwife. It's only then, at those moments, that I am tempted once again to not only read the book, but also to find her, possess her, steal her from him. Or him from her. Perhaps.

That first summer I thought I understood why he was reading the Flaubert again. I thought his knowledge of the book had grown rusty and he *needed* to do it. Well, perhaps there was some truth in that. Perhaps.

The weather that first year was surprisingly good. He had rented a room for us in a small hotel in Tenby, on the south west coast. The house was big, and while its entrance looked normal enough; a Georgian town house with a central front door, tall sash windows, a neat garden with a gate on an ordinary street in the middle of town, it was only when the landlady led us through to the back garden that I discovered its greatest secret.

It had crossed my mind that it was rather strange that she should want to show us the back of the house, but then as on the way she had shown us the dining room, the TV room and the bar; each room kitted out with a staggering array of kitsch nick-knacks, ornate cushions, fussy lace tablecloths and antimacassars, and faded reproductions of *The Haywain* and Hal's *Laughing Cavalier* and so on, I wasn't really surprised.

We followed her, nodding and smiling inanely, said 'ah' when she briefly opened a door to reveal a downstairs toilet; miniscule hand basin, avocado-coloured loo, fluffy pink mat circling its base, and a crocheted doll in loo roll-shaped crinoline overseeing proceedings from her podium above the cistern.

But then, and if I remember rightly the landlady hesitated theatrically, we came to a door at the back of the house.

'And through here,' she said, 'is the patio and the garden,' and she flung it open and stepped aside for us to proceed through it.

'Oh!' was all I could manage to say, for it was glorious. The lawn tilted down away from the house, and at its bottom edge, beyond an iron railing, was the immense and startling turquoise sea.

She led us down the path to a gate and with each step I got more of a sense of the house's precipitous place on the cliff top; the sudden drop to the vast and almost empty beach below.

'We have our own path,' she said, 'the steps lead all the way down to the sands.'

It was on those same twisting, turning, switchback, higgledy-piggledy, half stone, half concrete steps that he would propose to me a year later. I had lost my footing and he had caught me, stopped me from falling.

'Marry me,' he said. Just two words, as if it was a matter of great urgency. Or that's how I understood it at the time.

Now, thinking about it with the benefit of hindsight, I see that it could be construed as an order. And, a minor point perhaps, but I can't for the life of me remember if we were going up or going down the steps.

By the fourth year, in the same month, in the same town, in the same hotel, I was more usually than not winding my way down or up those steps alone.

The good weather was patchy that year; a day of overcast skies, followed by one of sunshine, then one of oppressive headache-inducing heat, then thunderstorms in the night.

He was writing a paper for a conference in the autumn.

'You don't mind do you?' he'd say. 'We'll go somewhere nice this evening? That new restaurant you mentioned?'

But then later, when I returned to our room it would be, 'Give me an hour, would you? I've had a sudden insight about the final chapter.'

Then one hour would turn into two, three, four and our meal would be ham sandwiches grudgingly provided by the landlady in her dressing gown and slippers, pink foam curlers in her hair, and the bread would be dry, and she would have no mustard even.

It all seemed temporary though, a mere glitch in the long happy marriage ahead. Besides which, I was, by then, trying for a baby. And if anyone wonders at that slip of the tongue, let me confess, that when I say *I*, I mean *I*. I had stopped taking my contraceptive pills and hadn't mentioned it, as I wanted to present him with a *fait accompli*.

But of course, it wasn't working. I couldn't quite believe it – all those years of being terrified of falling pregnant, all those years of pumping my body full of chemicals, or messing around with condoms, and now that I wanted it, my body was cheating me. And it did cross my mind once that maybe God or whatever was punishing me for trying to pull a fast one; for neglecting to tell my darling hubby about what I had planned. And even now I really don't quite know why I didn't mention it to him, or at least not at first.

Then one day, I can't quite remember when, I came back from the beach early. I had a headache; the beginnings of a dull ache in my lower back, a big angry pimple on my chin, and I felt thoroughly out of sorts; grumpy about everything, beginning with my own body and radiating out like beams of indignant anger at him and the world and history and human frailty and sin. Pre-menstrual tension, yes, a fat dollop of it, but salted by disappointment, as I knew that another dose of the curse was upon me and that I had yet again failed to conceive. All I had was nothing. Again.

When I came into the bedroom, he looked, at first, rather put out to see me, which did nothing to help my mood.

'Oh, don't worry,' I said, 'I won't disturb you. I'll just curl up on the bed and die very quietly.'

He hated sarcasm – called it the lowest form of wit. Though he quite naturally loved irony; personally I couldn't see the difference between the two. But anyway, I must have been at particularly low ebb, because the next thing I knew I was sobbing my eyes out, and anything but deep and heartfelt honesty was beyond me. 'You hate me,' I said, 'you're ashamed of me. You don't trust me. You're sorry you ever married me aren't you?'

Perhaps I should have carried on like this sooner, because it had a surprising effect; later that day over dinner, he finally told me about the terrible thing he had done all those years ago.

'My parents used to bring me here to visit my aunt. Then one year... there was a girl,' he said, and I found myself thinking of Emma Bovary, 'she lived very near here, just down by the harbour. She was, I think, seventeen or eighteen when we first met. I was about to go up to Cambridge. Over the course of that summer we fell madly and deeply in love. It was the first time, you see. We... I got quite carried away. Sometimes I think it was because of what I was reading at the time – the French novelists have always been suspected of having the power to corrupt. But that is no excuse, my behaviour was – is – unforgivable. There was a child, you see...' he looked away, as though he couldn't bear to look at me, 'and my choice was the scholarship to Cambridge, or an early and impecunious marriage... but I overlooked the fact that she had *no* choice.'

'Well,' I said, and then faltered; I had been about to say that it takes two to tango, but I realized I was speaking from a different age and a thoroughly different perspective.

'But,' he went on, 'Father and Mother were very quick to condemn her. They had heard talk of several beaus....'

I noticed how his language seemed to have reverted to some mannered Edwardian tract, how the words themselves seemed as tightly bound as if they were corseted.

'There was even talk that the child wasn't mine, that she had already been impregnated by the time I met her... and indeed the child was eventually born a little prematurely, but....'

He had his secrets. I had mine. Like Emma Bovary, sooner or later, we revert to form.

Sometime later I went to my doctor, then to a clinic, for tests and more tests. Nothing wrong with me, nothing at all.

'We should really do some tests on your partner,' the doctor said. She was kind. She indulged me, 'the problem with conception may be his.'

'No,' I said, 'I believe that he...' but then I stopped myself; maybe that baby from long ago hadn't been his, in which case he'd been torturing himself for nothing. Though I somehow suspected he would not be cheered by this news – no man wants to look like a fool.

The doctor was surprisingly elegant in her white coat; the stethoscope might have been some daring designer necklace. I trusted her. I told her that I didn't think he would agree to tests, and she shook her head gravely, and allowed that for some men this issue of fertility was too much tied up in their notions of what a real man is.

'Well,' she said, 'you have a dilemma. You must either reconcile yourself to a life without children, or you must end this relationship find a man who *can* give you children.'

Life is full of choices, a few of them better informed than others. I took *some* of the good doctor's advice, but not all of it.

Perhaps my husband was content to carry the burden of the past on his shoulders, atoning for his sin every summer by returning to the scene of the crime and rereading *Madame Bovary*, but I was getting older and more impatient than ever for something more tangible than a memory or a story. I wanted a child.

This one page I tore from Flaubert's book; I took a lover.

This year the steps up from the beach are a bit much for someone in my condition. But that's okay. I like to stay in our room; I like to watch my clever husband read; and now and then, once in a while, he'll recite a few pages aloud.

And while he speaks I see glimpses of Emma's white hands, her almond nails and dark eyes. Beguiling though she is, I still can't quite believe her gestation was so slow; five words an hour? Life is faster than that. Was mercurial, even then.

If the baby is a girl, he wants to call her 'Emma' and I've agreed. He deserves that much at least.

The Pendulum

She waited for him in the twilight of the children's playground. She sat on the swing with each hand gripping the heavy chain that held it suspended, but kept both of her feet on the ground and her bottom on the edge of the seat. She rocked gently to and fro by flexing one knee and rolling on the ball of one foot.

Waited. Watched. Rocked. Resisted swinging.

A year ago the playground was for play and had been down all the years of her remembering. As she grew up so she had mastered the art of swinging. Learning first to hold on and be pushed, then to swing herself, and finally to swing higher and higher and to leap off at the highest point of the forward swing. To leap into the arching void and land with two feet down and running. The moment she had mastered all the tricks of the playground, the speed, the daring, the reckless disregard for heights, that was the moment she had to give it all up. Forsake it for lolling around the record shop, shoplifting cheap lipsticks from supermarkets and smoking furtive roll-ups in foul-smelling toilets and back alleys.

She missed the playground, the thrilling sensations of spiralling, rocking, swooping movement and the shared games of the imagination, the gasping whispers of pretend, the running and chasing, the high careless laughter echoing off concrete paving and walls.

She missed it all, but resisted swinging.

The setting sun that evening had a sort of glory about it and cast a red celebratory hue over everything.

She grew aware of the sun sinking lower in the sky, the lengthening shadows and the dying light, and the trees a black intricate tracery of leaves and branches against the scarlet flooded sky.

She guessed at the time, as it was her habit to go without a watch despite her parents' nagging and the Christmas and birthday presents of watches and watches and watches.

To be young, she thought, meant to live without time. Or at least to exist outside of it in a place called love or freedom or weightlessness.

And still it grew darker and still she resisted the temptation to swing.

There was no sign of him yet and she knew that he was unlikely to come strolling along the pavement. Instead, like last time, and the time before that, he would come out of the darkness in the woods at the edge of the park, a moving shadow almost swallowed up by the greater shadows of the trees.

The subterfuge was only partly necessary. His garden backed onto those woods and so he came that way, clambering through the broken fence, weaving between the weeds into the sheltering trees, then into the park itself.

He was the music teacher's son. Six feet and one inch tall, rake thin but with broad shoulders. An impossibly long back as though he had an extra disk or three in his spinal column. Low slim hips. Sinewy arms and the long fine fingers of a pianist, except that the hands were happier when wrapped around a pair of bruised and splintering drumsticks, than stepping daintily over the cold bones of a piano's keys.

His teeth were crooked as he skipped or refused the orthodontist's jaw-numbing attentions.

On his chest, in the centre, a diamond-shaped thicket of sparse hair. On his thumb a silver ring. Fingernails chewed to ragged redness.

His blue eyes wore the far off gaze of the myopic dreamer. He would not wear glasses.

His father (although it is hard to believe that this man has contributed to the boy's gene pool) is five-feet seven with a cherub's face half buried beneath a bushy red-tinged beard. He is employed at the Girl's School. Her school. He is one of those teachers who is neither sexy nor scary, but is considered in some ways comical. He is for the most part mild-mannered and kind, and this is taken for weakness.

Sometimes he lets down his guard and stands before the class conducting the curling and jagged notes that come pouring out of the cassette deck. His enthusiasm lets him down, 'Ah, Mozart,' the music teacher says with undisguised wonder. 'Wolfgang Amadeus Mozart, 1759 to 1791. How does a Mozart happen?' He asks this with hands reaching up to God, to fate, to Freud, to Beelzebub. No one answers.

He plays the comic duet of Papigano and Papigana from the Magic Flute. This surprises the assembled class, the music has not the expected bulk of boredom to it, they are not drowning in the ennui of Handel's Water Music. Instead, here is a comical tinny, twinkly sound like something from a children's programme.

'My son used to do a little dance to this,' the music teacher says and she is horrified that her entire class has to hear this intimate memory from her boyfriend's childhood. Not that anyone knows that her boyfriend is the music teacher's son.

The night gathers in the shadows, knots together the leaves and branches of the trees, creeps upon the grass with stealth, turning green into darker green and then to blackness.

She resists swinging, but through the rolling of her toes she has found an old enthusiasm in the sheltering private dusk. If she could remain undiscovered then perhaps she would allow herself the old pleasure. But she will not, she cannot, because soon he will come.

Soon he will come, loping silent through the blind dew, metamorphosing from the bunched and knotted night into himself, into the known one, the loved one.

Even after he has reached her, is standing close

enough to touch, he will retain a sort of shifty awkward strangeness.

This will last for a few minutes, this strangeness, and she will still her gentle swinging as if to mark his arrival, her arrival at this moment of maturity, the meeting of lover with lover.

Yet the awkwardness never quite departs. She is forever arriving, recording, reminding herself that this is *her*, vulnerable in the darkness, raw as a newly budded breast, as pleasurable and memorable as lips first kissed and first born to the too true meeting of their lips in the new kisses of grown up love.

And she waits.

She does not swing the swing, but searches that infinite blackness with eyes that despite their keenness, their hope, their love cannot make his shape evolve.

In those moments she is afraid.

Afraid enough to still her gentle rolling and let her ears play against the void that is as much without humanity as it is without light and sound. And just as she is about to give up, just as her desire to swing finally truly dies, then he comes, at first as a distant sound and then, as she turns to the sound, as a human shape.

Tonight he comes from the wrong direction. Draws near, says 'hey.'

'Oh,' she says, 'oh, where have you been?'

'Pub,' he says. One word and a broad loose grin explaining the route, the lateness, the beery smell.

What is she meant to do or say now? How do the matters of men and women unravel themselves when the rules are broken? What is the difference between them in this young night and the older world that settles in for the night beyond the curtained windows, on sofas, in the blue flickering light from the TV set.

She has to think. To recover herself. To reassert what she started out with, which has now changed. So again, she begins to slowly roll her toe against the wood chips underfoot. To pretend that she barely notices him.

'Here I am,' she thinks, 'just me, in the night, in the playground, untouchable, a girl enjoying a ride on a swing.'

Then as soon as she has been so bold as to lift two feet off the ground, he has stepped in front of the swing and grabbed the two chains that hold it, so that the swing is stilled. But below his hands the momentum keeps going and she crashes into him.

He falls to his knees, absorbs the weight of her flight, sucks the violence of it into that bruiseless painless half-drunken young body of his. And then he reaches for her, at first clumsily, then with surety. His hands touch her face. His fingers are both tender and tentative and cold to the touch.

How did he learn that? She wonders. How did he invent this gesture? How could he know how effective it would be despite the beer and confusion.

His two hands holding her face as a knight holds the Holy Grail.

'Drink to me only with thine eyes!'

That was the stupid song their old music teacher made them sing, that his father, the new teacher sneered at.

'I think I love you,' he says.

258

And there it is, the phrase that stands alone, bare as a bone illuminated by the last fragile light of the moon. But with that curious adjunct 'I *think* I love you'.

For her the 'I think' makes it more real, or perhaps more artful.

Now she would like to swing away, to swing on happiness in treble time, but he's holding her there, fixed in the moment like a spider trapped beneath a glass.

But no, not like a spider under a glass, but something infinitely more beautiful and rare; a butterfly or orchid.

And then he laughs. A stupid Beavis and Butthead kind of laugh. One she's never heard before. Something else that's new, that he's just learned in the pub, in the company of men.

What she does not know is that he hadn't expected silence from her after his confession. What she could not know is that he went to the pub in order to learn these new words. Or not to learn them, but rather to discover how to release them as they had been flapping around in his head like a bird trapped in a sealed room for a long time now.

They neither of them understand the threads of misunderstanding that separate them. The misunderstanding that hangs like a disintegrating curtain in a deserted house, holding back the day's light, smearing the room beyond with a closeted darkness.

He falls back on humour, those words of love were only laughs; light irony, lingering ponytail pulling, the boy teasing girl kind of love. Or even lies. The sort of lies he has heard among men. Lies about telling women what they want to hear. The magic 'I love you' that is a cold hand snaking its way inside tight underwear, that is clumsy fingers struggling with the fastening of a bra.

But what would be the point of that lie now, when secretly in the dark places of the park and the graveyard they have lain their sweet and innocent selves aside like two perfect ghosts?

She used to think it would be terribly sad to die young, and sadder still to die a virgin; to pass from this earthly existence without ever knowing its most profound joy, that of being in love and being one flesh, white and goose-bumped in the silvery moonlight.

'C'mon,' he says, slurring very slightly and clumsily reaching for her.

He should be holding her hand. That would be the good romantic thing to do, but instead he has caught hold of her wrist and so her arm has become the useless passive limb of the captive.

He leads her away from the swings, across the black grass, into the trees and halfway there a part of her resists. This is like one of her nightmares, a stranger dragging her into the forest. Bluebeard with his castle of many rooms and the secret chamber where he keeps the girls' hair. Those precious hanks of silver and gold. The chestnut and the raven-black, bloodied at the root, each hanging from its own butcher's hook on the white wall. Soft hair, cold steel, blood as red as roses.

She is his secret. That is why he usually falls backward from the night, getting artfully through his back garden and meeting her only in the swing park after dark.

Tonight drink has tumbled him into the open, a grouse

raised by beaters, when he falls to earth again he will be altered.

This is an accumulation of misunderstanding, spiralling out of control. It is music building to a crescendo, the pianist's fingers flying ever leftward, ever heavier on the darker, deeper notes that wait there.

None of this is beautiful or romantic or pure. It is stumbling and clumsy, not love at all as she imagines it.

He has a new idea, a new purpose. He is giddy with the brilliance of it; the acutely ordinary simplicity of this. He is taking her home to meet his parents. His parents, who tonight are listening to a live performance of Wagner's *Tristan and Isolde* on Radio 3. His mother likes to paint little abstract watercolours while she listens. Her pictures are like small bright jewels, bedazzling. His father might follow the score or merely close his eyes in some heavenly reverie.

The boy thinks his parents are weird. Seriously weird, they don't even own a TV, but somehow, for some reason, after all the subterfuge, he suddenly wants them to meet *his love*.

But his love, reduced now in his mind to that thin wrist which his hands tightly circle, is unsettled by confusion. His earlier laugh has stabbed her heart and what pours out from the wound is a stubborn juice, bile-coloured and streaked with old anger.

In the darkest part of the thicket where the ground is spongy and mushrooms grow, she stops moving and wrenches her hand free. The violence of it burns her skin and that increases her anger. She hears his cry of surprise, the confusion of a half-voiced word.

'Heh...'

She hears him stumbling awkwardly amongst the branches, the snapped twig sounds as he finds his feet.

She runs back towards the brightly-coloured slides and swings in their shades of night grey. She runs past them without stopping, climbs the low fence, then races down the road until she turns a corner and the playground is out of sight. Only then does she slow her pace, and inspect her wrist, though there is nothing wrong with it. Not really.

The music stops. A cloud uncovers the moon. The wind rises from the east and finds that it is just strong enough to move the row of dangling swings an inch or so, from here to there, from there to here, to and fro. Just enough to make them creak. To make night music; that no one hears.

Acknowledgements

With thanks to my editor Gwen Davies, my publisher Richard Davies, lloyd robson, and also to Katy Train for all her help.

This book was written with the help of a writer's bursary from The Welsh Academy and a grant from the Author's Society, both of which are greatly appreciated.

Some of these stories appeared in the following publications: *Urban Welsh*; *Mirror, Mirror*; *Ghosts of the Old Year*; *Quare Fellas*; *Big Issue Cymru*; *Cambrensis* and *New Welsh Review*.